Do Not Go to the Jungle

Shihabuddin Poithumkadavu was born in 1963 in Kannur, north Kerala. He is one of Malayalam's leading fiction writers. He has been awarded the most prestigious prizes for literature in Malayalam: the Kerala Sahitya Akademi Award, the P. Padmarajan prize, the V.T. Bhattatiripad prize and the Abudhabi Malayali Samajam Award, among others.

Shihabuddin's working life began at the age of fifteen when he dropped out of school and began to work as a cleaner in a hotel. Since then he worked multiple jobs—as a helper in wedding feasts, a waiter in a restaurant, an ironing boy, a cleaner in a lorry, subscription-collector for the local merchants' association, by-stander in a hospital, proofreader, timber loader, house painter, wood polisher, sand loader, cashier in a restaurant, nightwatchman in a saw mill, and so on. However, he continued his school education and went on to earn a college degree, after which he worked in different capacities in the media as journalist, script-writer, and editor in Dubai and Kerala. He has published thirty-eight books in Malayalam and his oeuvre includes short stories, novels, poetry, essays and memoirs. His work has been translated into Hindi, Tamil, English and Arabic.

His first story appeared in print in 1982, after which he was widely recognised to be a new and electrifying voice that challenged accepted aesthetic practices in writing. His first collection of short stories appeared soon after and received much praise from the doyens of Malayalam literature, including Kamala Das and T. Padmanabhan. Most of his books have run into multiple editions, with the sales of each one crossing 10,000 copies. His stories have been prescribed by the Kerala State Education Board, the University of Calicut, the Mahatma Gandhi University and the University of Kerala, in their syllabi.

J. Devika is a researcher and teacher at the Centre for Development Studies, Thiruvananthapuram. She has translated the works of many literary authors including K.R. Meera, Sara Joseph, Unni R. and several others from Malayalam to English.

Do Not Go to the Jungle

Shihabuddin Poithumkadavu

TRANSLATED FROM THE MALAYALAM
BY J. DEVIKA

eka

eka

First published in English as *Do Not Go to the Jungle* in 2021 by Eka, an imprint of Westland Publications Private Limited

Published in 2023 by Eka, an imprint of Westland Books, a division of Nasadiya Technologies Private Limited

No. 269/2B, First Floor, 'Irai Arul', Vimalraj Street, Nethaji Nagar, Allappakkam Main Road, Maduravoyal, Chennai 600095

Westland, the Westland logo, Eka and the Eka logo are the trademarks of Nasadiya Technologies Private Limited, or its affiliates.

Copyright © Shihabuddin Poithumkadavu, 2021
Translation copyright © J. Devika, 2021

ISBN: 9789395767989

10 9 8 7 6 5 4 3 2 1

This is a work of fiction. Names, characters, organisations, places, events and incidents are either products of the author's imagination or used fictitiously.

Typeset by Jojy Philip, New Delhi 110 015

Printed at Nutech Print Services - India, Faridabad

CONTENTS

Translator's Note   vii

The Fox in the Sawmill   1

Malabar Express   8

Do Not Go to the Jungle, Little One!   17

The Horse   29

Beast to the Slaughter   33

Palanquins that Run Backwards   39

A Page in the History of Evolution   41

Bodheswaran   50

Beast   65

The Son of Joseph   74

Yakshiscars   78

Houses, Too, Are Alive   89

A Hospital Visit   98

The Holes that the Earth Begot   100

Prisoners of the Taj Mahal   106

All Alone in this Railway Station   114

History-as-Maya   121

The Lunatic   132

The Flaming Pillow   143

Winter   147

Isa   156

TRANSLATOR'S NOTE

If I were asked to name five of Kerala's national treasures from the Malayalam literary universe, the name of Shihabuddin Poithumkadavu would figure in the list, and on the higher side. His writing is not merely good—it is challenging. Like a true work of art, the opacity of which invites us to meditate on it and create not just meaning but intense affect, Shihabuddin's text leads us on strange, unfamiliar paths visible only to the underdog. The translator's greatest responsibility here is to transfer into the target language the vertigo-inducing power of Shihabuddin's storytelling.

These texts are hard to translate: there is often no stable first-person in them; prose and poetry appear and disappear erratically; Sufi meditations on the Void and surreal narrations coalesce and separate to produce unfamiliar senses of space and movement; tenses shift abruptly, disorienting one's sense of time; bizarre metaphors and similes jump over or break set images and connections. In order to craft a mirror capable of revealing simultaneously the ugliness of effete religiosity and stunted faith, and the blind pitilessness of bureaucratised state power, Shihabuddin reworks in a Sufi imagination the dystopic images that abound in his times. However, the glowing frame in which this mirror is mounted is, no doubt, a deep and abiding compassion. To put it short, not your cozy, easy realism, this.

Many of these texts, then, are fine, sophisticated, compassionate critiques of power in its many manifestations. Take, for instance, '*Yakshippandu*' (translated as 'Yakshiscars' in this volume). It is undoubtedly one of the most exquisite and enlightening meditations on desire in Malayalam. Set in a fictitious town called 'Madampi' (meaning 'tyrant'), a place of bustling trade established by a colonial master, the tale revolves around a woman who stirs up men's sexual passions. She arrives and leaves mysteriously, and offers pleasure freely to all men, only to leave them drained and ailing. Who she is—a blood-sucking vampire or just a skilled whore—no one knows. That she will not be possessed by a single man leads to tragedy—and her truth is revealed. The *yakshi*'s lifeless body is found to be scarred and covered with wounds, and its beauty, revealed to be a mere illusion. Indeed, this pitiful corpse is the handiwork of violent, grasping patriarchal power—ultimately weak and cowardly, for it murders that which it cannot fully master. But desire is deathless. It escapes the bounds of the town of Madampi and into the universe—and is still female. It is hardly a surprise, then, that the story itself breaks the bounds of prose and soars into the skies of poetry at its culmination. Desire is almost worshipped as deathless and female-bodied. The translator's skill is truly tested at this intense climax: the *yakshi* as desire is both a force and female, both 'it' and 'woman'.

But such soaring that borders on prayer is rare in Shihabuddin's stories. For the most part, they are nightmarish or horror-inducing. Shihabuddin himself has remarked elsewhere that his stories are mostly horror stories, and one of his novellas is subtitled a 'socio-horror' novel. In other words, his stories are of powerless individuals, mostly male but excluded from dominant masculinity, trapped in the labyrinths of bureaucratised modernity and watching with horror the sight of their selves being rent apart or turning unfamiliar. These 'non-men' are very often close to the non-human worlds despoiled and tyrannised by human civilisation. But they may also be persecuted and broken revolutionaries, the wretched poor and the mad, who are preyed upon by the irrational fears of the powerful. Their witnessing and narration, however, constitute acts of subversion and resistance. Many of Shihabuddin's stories, however, also take apart dominant masculinity with incomparable precision ('Beast' and 'History-as-Maya' in this volume, for instance), but within a frame of compassion still. The translator cannot escape the obligation to peer into Shihabuddin's mirror that refuses to reflect back the veil of hypocrisy that shields the world's ugliness. Indeed, without it, the translation of these texts is well-nigh impossible.

I thank Shihabuddin for letting me do this, and for patiently answering my questions. Minakshi Thakur's meticulous editing, as usual, has helped me immensely. I thank the proofreader, too, for her superb work. Finally, starting with my teacher M. Gangadharan, I thank all those who urged me to hold these marvellous texts close, and to enter them with wonder and love.

J. Devika

THE FOX IN THE SAWMILL

Opening the gate made of old saw blades, I peeped in. The expansive world inside fell on my eyes as a freshly-wrought sight.

The sawmill was in the middle of an island some six or seven acres wide. It lay prostrate on the ground like a decrepit, enormous old man. It was bound by thickets towards the western side near where a veritable hill of sawdust rested. Beyond it flowed the river, on the banks of which tiny crabs scurried about, always scared and harried. Night was creeping up slowly from the river's mouth and edging its way up and across the water's vast spread. I saw that darkness had arrived earlier than usual, and stood waiting by the outhouse beside the sawmill. As I stepped into the compound holding my packed dinner, leaden silence and loneliness, as heavy as Death's gigantic bosom, were waiting for me as usual. Those who have known this life will recognise it. The life of a solitary nightwatchman always unfolds under Death's dark blanket.

It was during these sombre days that I first met him. A fox. It's possible that he had slipped out of hiding by mistake, or maybe he was helpless because the thicket had no more food left to offer—I don't know which of the two had drawn him out. But he gradually became a familiar sight. This place is called Parappankaadu—actually *paranna-kaadu*—meaning 'sprawling forest'.

I can imagine much better than you what the life of a fox must be like after the forest got chopped down. Because that is quite like the life of the nightwatchman, cast out by society.

I began to feel that our meeting, just before the dusk deepened, was no coincidence. The way he stood still, unblinking, watching me as I approached, his eyes sifting frantically through his memory—where, where have I seen this human before—until I was up close. The way he disappeared, quick as a bolt of lightning, when alarmed by the proximity. His thoughtful look once again, from the top of the deserted sawmill's platform, as he perched there with his head held high ... After many days I realised, it was searching for itself in the lineages of evolution itself, of civilisation, of human dominance.

I could read the thoughts glinting and vanishing in his eyes: Is it this human, this fruit of evolution, who set my forests on fire? Is it he who tore me apart from my mate? Is it this human who forged between us a gulf so enormous that we will never couple again?

I began to reach out to him.

Look, I am nowhere in the annals of your past. In any case, why are you adamant even now about not leaving the forest, why do you resist being tamed, why do you still cling to this ancient and wasted grey? Can I make a pet of you? The forest—we humans have cleared all of it. Why do you not accept this reality?

Shake off your rusty old notions. I can find you a female if you want. You can copulate as much as you wish then. But on one condition: You must move into the realm of domesticated creatures. Don't you see the town growing! The forest's darkness, its mighty stupas, are collapsing one by one. Even the laws of the jungle have been tamed into domesticated animals!

For whom do you lead this life in hiding?

Look at me, for instance. All my legacies were plundered by outsiders. The outsiders penetrated us, stayed inside us as an invisible force, as fear, as conflagration, as tension—in ways that made it impossible for humans to reach out to one another. We gave up very quickly. Not one of History's agonising tail-ends have survived. But one good came of this surrender—people got back their lives. Don't ask me what kind of lives. The books I studied said, do not chop down the forest. We learned much about Nature and its science. But today, I watch over the insensate slumber of this sawmill—out cold from tearing into Nature all day long, screeching and snarling—so that I can buy my rations. I have a social life, a family. But what about you? Hey, why're you staring? I know from your look that you have no plans of surrendering; you want to continue being that clever story from Aesop's Fables. Clever indeed! What use is fame, my friend? What you think to be cleverness, is a life of hiding—a foolish solitude. Why don't you see that no one will be with you? Neither the crabs in this river nor the small birds. Do you manage to quell your hunger? Do you know everything is about to end? When you can find no more food one day, will it be easy to slip into town fast enough?

Think. I can save you. Slowly, very slowly, I will prove to you that you are a town-creature. I will make sure no one hurts you.

End this damned aloneness! It is nothing but a scrounge-trip into one's own self—well, sort of. Tattered ideas. The terrible embers of insecurity—you suffer these and much more, all by yourself. Give up the obduracy, my friend! If you don't want to come to town, then join me, in this little space—be with the human you can trust the most on this earth. I'll bring you cooked rice, and lots of different kinds of food. You don't have to even wag your tail in gratitude. I know that your tail with its thick coat of hair won't yield so soon. It's all right to take it slow. It is easy.

The fox stood still, staring me down like a learned sage. But he did not take even a single step to lessen the distance between us.

Very late into that night, I heard his long-winded call. To his mate. A sad, futile, pathetic call. Lamenting in search of the clan, I'm-still-here-I'm-still-here-I'm-still-here, it cried. A song that caressed itself and laid to rest its own desire. If that call wasn't a song after all, then who knows, maybe he is a poet? Crafting a long poem in response to my rather long address earlier that evening, and reciting it? A sharp and biting retort. But then, what humans can know is strictly limited. And me, I know even less.

I remembered him when I was packing dinner to come to work the next day. I packed some rice for him too, mixing it with appetisingly-scented fish curry. I was packing my hope—how long can he hold back? When the forest itself was losing its foundations one by one, where could *he* hide what was given to him as inheritance—his cleverness? I had observed that the fox looked terribly wan and thin lately. That there wasn't enough food was evident. The huge factory that had come up recently on the other side of the riverbank was polluting the river viciously. Much of the fish had migrated, seeking cleaner waters. The rest of them had died and floated up on the river like a complaint written to God above. The crabs, too, had been drained of life.

Hey fox, the little birds that used to swoop down to snatch the twigs floating on the river will come no more. The snails in the mangroves have all given up the ghost, thanks to the poison from the factory. All around you, the town has woken up. Today, in the hollow of the granite quarry on the Parappankunnu hill, where your forefathers once frolicked, Blade Rajappan, that petty usurer, runs a medical college! Hey fox, no life will you find in that tiny little thicket which is fast dying. No more prey will you sight. No more mates are written in your destiny.

Look at me, at my thighs. On them is the mark of the Emergency, that rolled over this land like the logs the police used on political prisoners back then. The policemen, like Jayaram Padikkal and Lakshmana, who rolled out the diktats in cells stinking of shit at police camps. All that's left of my turbulent youth are these dried-up wounds, these depressions, dug into the surface of my thighs like channels. Only the red, blue and black marks of the lathi, on which my mother rubbed medicated oil and her tears, have disappeared. Am I not aware that in order to bring logs to this sawmill, the axe should tear into the heart of the forest?

I gave in. For people like us, life is meant to be nothing but defeat. Some people think even now that defeats may yet be victories, at least occasionally. Lucky ones! I don't belong to that set. But, hey fox, for how long can we continue this way? How long will you protect the bequest of genes that thrash and scratch inside your brain incessantly? Please listen to me. All these lonely journeys, these thoughts from all kinds of crooked angles, these worries, dilemmas—all are meaningless.

I'm not calling you to surrender. Maybe we could call this a state of easing-into-everyday. Or how about calling it getting-normal? What matters is not the adjective but the condition. The natural course through which this tattered life of yours flows reminds me of my own unquiet ocean of despair. How threateningly this life speaks to us! The tightened fist of reality is in our face, it never lets us rest. When you call out loud into the moonlight, you dream that someday another fox will reach your side. You hope that your wild home will flourish, and that there will be enough prey. At times you even think that you are a trickster. But a moment later, it dawns upon you that yours is a fool's life. Do you know, like you, your cleverness is orphaned too? It lacks wile. When a tired bird falls into your hands by chance, you grab it, your fur rising in a feeling of triumph. But on the days when not even a tiny crab comes your way, you sink into the void of diffidence. Many a time, you are the humble one who did not get a chance in this world full of the impulse to dominate. My dear fox, come to town. Leave behind this accursed thicket of your sense of self; get used to being without it. The town beckons you.

I see myself in you, and so, for the comfort of my soul, I will help you. Here, start with this fish-curry-scented rice. There's everything we need in town. You can have it all. Never ask, however, for an expression of the soul's instincts. Give in, give in. Cut yourself off from history; the present alone is real. The town calls you—rise, my dear fox, from your grubby pits of dismay! Here is your packet of rice. Do not be so full of bitter suspicion; do not stand so far away and stare. You can maybe eat it later too, after I leave.

The fox, however, was still running further and further away, zigzagging and sneakily turning back to look. When the faint light of the dying dusk fell on the leaves, he disappeared into the thicket.

But I can see. Those eyes staring hard from inside the thicket can only be yours. The pupils of those eyes that scratch at sight so hard and so long—what can be filling them, brimming in them again and again, but thoughts?

MALABAR EXPRESS

The earth revolves by itself on the orbit that goes around the sun. The wind, the rain, the seasons—they all have the same rhythm, the same order. Nature does not like anyone obstructing its laws. But the calculations of humans—earthlings—can go wrong any time. That's the joke Nature's played on us!

If this weren't the case, how could one explain why Comrade Aayiram Kalathil Govindan—Govindan-of-a-thousand-arenas—ended up in the ordinary compartment of the Malabar Express?

Aayiram Kalathil Govindan is always surrounded by slogans, always encircled by supporters, always at press conferences, always in front of the microphone. He can't even steal a nap unnoticed; His acolytes won't let Him. Tender coconut water to drink; meals according to a prescribed menu; check-ups in between; the end-of-the-year massage; special vehicles for bumpy roads to protect His back, which once took the brunt of police violence.

A thin, aged comrade would inevitably run up from somewhere to carry His bags; another comrade wearing a humble, soiled *kaili* made sure the serving leaf was freshly cut whenever He sat down to eat; a third comrade with dark *beedi*-stained lips would be ever ready to climb up the coconut tree whenever He felt thirsty—this comrade had never read *Das Capital* even once (indeed—in every district, these comrades had exactly the same face!).

Yes, He did have the facilities to enjoy solitude in any kind of crowded situation. They had never let Him travel in a train without air-conditioning. In the drama that passed off as protest, enacted when the party was in the opposition, He was protected from stones and lathis by that sad thing, the Body of the People. The officials appointed by the ruling party sent His daughter to bourgeois countries for higher education, despite his many objections ... He had prayed that His sons don't grow up to be thugs. But they became just that. Against His staunch opposition, they entered the corporate world and reached great heights. Now and then, this plunged Him into deep crises of the conscience. The first time: this is not right. Next time: who is right? And still later: why seek what's right just all alone? After this, Comrade Aayiram Kalathil Govindan rarely had a moment to Himself. He flies from party meetings to strategy discussions to demonstrations to inaugurating protest pickets, and from Delhi to Trivandrum, and from Trivandum to Delhi. Occasionally, to Kolkata. From north to south in Kerala and back.

In rare moments of solitude, He slipped away to the beach and watched the sunset. Those are His moments of deep nostalgia. The way the sky grew steadily red—that was like His inner world as a child, cut and served up in so many pieces. The sea's scream—a lover from yore, who fell off somewhere along the way (or was she abandoned?), a beloved-in-memory. The days of revolution, yet to come, thrust its arms and legs and wailed like an infant orphaned and abandoned somewhere in a corner of His mind. He wiped off the tears with a khadi towel. When dusk fell, He walked back to the white car and the driver waiting in it. For a long time, He was silent. And, now, how did *this* happen? How did He end up clasping hard the long steel hand-rail? His confused compass? His muddled sense of direction?

Also, the Malabar Express left rather quickly, did it not? Where is my suitcase? Why, this is not the AC compartment! The large iron door that clanged shut behind me, which cell does it belong to? In this general compartment, filled with the stench of urine, brewed in *beedi*-smoke, nothing seems visible—it is so dark! Suddenly, the train entered a tunnel, almost drowning the ear and killing it with sound.

After a few breathless moments, Comrade Aayiram Kalathil Govindan regained His senses. He had got into the wrong compartment. This is not the AC, this is the general compartment. Not enough light in here. Stuffed with passengers. The urine-stench oozed and spread till it touched one's blanked-out consciousness. Below the dim light, on the dirty wall, someone had scratched the names of much-coveted women with a pencil stub. Below it, the obscene *padmasana* of the oppressed, men jerking off (in truth, this is solitary prayer, to one's own tool, what else could it be?). Comrade Govindan hesitated to lean on the wall. These naked images are not yet dry, said an absurdity that popped up right then. They are waiting for a rebirth of the cum. You need to get a hold first. He got it. Now He wouldn't be shoved all around the compartment and beyond. But why was this hot breeze that kept going round and round in the compartment cooking up so much stench? He feared it may linger on Him in the party meeting the next day. Suddenly, He felt a wave of anger rising within Him with a snarl. Better to get off at the next station and re-board? But how to push aside this sweat-soaked-shirt-clad man in front who was blocking His sight completely? And what was wriggling up His right leg? Not memories of hiding from the police; not a snake or scorpion. A man who was sleeping on a piece of newspaper laid out on the floor had moved a bit, that was all! He heard Fate's seemingly never-ending whistle, both helpless and drunk on itself. The train shook for a moment as if protesting that its wheels could not take the speed; it seemed to have slipped off the iron track, hit the ground, and then got back on the rails to speed on, driven by some new rational thought. But Comrade Aayiram Kalathil Govindan had hit a hurdle and stopped. The man in the sweat-soaked cheap Terylene shirt (yes, of the same value, he and his shirt) was actually dozing. The train would stop at that less-crowded station for barely a minute—He remembered the local secretary Comrade Ramesan telling him so. Many a time before, He had thought the Malabar Express to be a wonderful night-train. It sang words that smothered the AC's hum. Its wheels that composed music for those words; the high- and low-pitched music in the shivers and quivers of the speeding, like in sex. The memory of falling asleep in the AC compartment, hugging all that coolness, came to the Comrade as a sensuous memory.

In truth, this is all Comrade Ramesan's fault. He had agreed to come to the station. He had been pulled up two times earlier for serious dereliction of duty. And the pall of boredom on his face these days had also been noticed. Let me get to Thiruvananthapuram ... where is the train now? Can't recollect the next station ... What's the way to end this tedious hell? Pull the chain? Will they charge the penalty once they know it was me? But even for that, this sweaty devil should move a little! I am Aayiram Kalathil Govindan, move aside. The Comrade tried to shove him out of the way, trying to convey these words silently. But to no avail. There was no space for even a needle in there. But hell, who's this sweat-soaked tall fellow who blocks my way? Hey you, move aside, the Comrade commanded, nearly roaring. This fellow knows nothing about my clout! Party members who love me call me 'A.K. Gopalan Junior'. If AKG had not arrived earlier in history, those initials would have fitted me perfectly! 'Comrade Govindan' does not sound as grand as 'Comrade AKG'. How I wish I too could share that name!

In this way, all of the party's past and present passed like a flash of lightning through Comrade Govindan's mind. He had become an MLA, then a minister; He retained high office in the party. The name 'AKG' isn't bigger than that! There's something wrong in desiring it too. The times have changed. The script is different. All talk about the old times is just desperate nostalgia. The only thing that doesn't change is change itself. But, why can't this devil standing in front change his position? Hey you, move, shift! Comrade Govindan shouted again. Let me get a bit of light! The man in front turned around. His face was impassive and pale. There's no light anywhere, he murmured, without a trace of emotion. Comrade Govindan reeled as though He had been slapped. You're trying to teach me? As He prepared a befitting retort, the shards of light from a train running towards them in the opposite direction scattered in the compartment. Comrade Govindan noticed that the man was blind. He had two holes in the place of eyes. When the other train disappeared screaming, the eternal hidden life of darkness came right back. The man looked nowhere and scratched his ear with his free hand like an autistic child. How to stop this train? I can't stand anymore in the middle of all this dirt. This train's been speeding so long and screaming non-stop. Pushing aside the odour that was spitting fire inside his nostrils, Govindan looked around. The sights in the compartment began to appear before His eyes one by one.

What was the general compartment of this Malabar Express but hell on which moonlight fell? Six people sat huddled together, dozing on a seat meant for four. A farmer's family stood in the passage, their legs aching. One of its members had turned bald from chemotherapy. Anaemic and deaf, their individuality swallowed up by others, they stood there like useless, dense emptiness, dozing briefly on the handcuffs of their fate for some time, and waking briefly in discontent, brushing against the sitting man's shoulder. On the floor, on newspaper-sheets spread out, a loader's family lay asleep. Their three-year-old daughter woke up and started wailing loudly. The Comrade was astonished. People who could sleep on the floor covered with *beedi*-stubs, food waste, heaps of dust, wetness—people pushed down on the ground, knocked down on the floor, now used to it! Two people sat, backs turned to each other, on the luggage carrier barely a foot wide. In between, the wind that had managed to get in—like an absurdity—when the train was crossing a river, was trying to blow the spread newspapers off the floor. But the newspapers held their ground. The newspapers are with the reviled and the persecuted—the thought shot through Comrade Govindan's mind. It helped Him regain his sense of self: I am Comrade Aayiram Kalathil Govindan. I appear at least two times in the newspapers every week, with photos and statements. But not a single passenger had recognised him! The Malabar Express began to reach medium speed once it crossed the river. Then it slowed down and finally stopped. A cool, fresh feeling quickly summoned Him. But it was fruitless. Comrade Aayiram Kalathil Govindan could not get out of the closed compartment. He pushed aside the blind man and lunged hard at the handle, trying to open the door. It responded in the language of iron: silence. I want out, I want to get out of this hell. I am an old man, I am weak. My legs are swollen from all this standing. My knee is almost crumbling in pain. Please, can someone help? Please tell me at least, which station is this?

The voice that had drowned tens of thousands of people in their own thunderous applause, the Hercules who had dug channels through which votes flowed swiftly into the ballot-box, 'Junior AKG', who had smashed the cheek of the attacker who had raised a hand to Him—what happened to His voice now? What swift swelling of diffidence had arisen now in His throat? Good God, no one is getting on or off. What's happened to this compartment? What is that little light outside? What is this compartment—that no one ever gets on or off—if not a massive coffin buried somewhere in a static time beyond the senses? Getting past the sweat-drenched blind man, Comrade Aayiram Kalathil Govindan rode through one of the most horrendous and disheartening crises of the self ever faced by History. Just a step. Just one more! This night-train packed with layer after layer of corpses is immobilising me. A feverish fit swooped out of His brain. Disguised, it approached His so-unexpectedly-stalled life like a beautiful *yakshi*, a she-ghoul that asked for lime-paste before it devoured its victims.

The train began to move again. The gloomy interior of the compartment began to become a little more live. The Comrade tried to shake off the many forms of inertness in which He was trapped. Soaking in perspiration, tired to the bone, aching all over, His life stood still, all possibilities of communication closed. He felt that the masses which had roared in welcome and sheer adoration had abandoned Him in just a minute. He was just another hapless passenger. If that is so, I will die standing thus. The newspapers will carry the headline: The Commander of the Poor Passes Away in the Compartment of the Poor. The masses at the head of the funeral procession, leading the red-flag-wrapped hearse! Its tour of the length and breadth of Kerala! What's the use of fame once you are dead? Fame after death is like a child your wife bore you with someone else—Comrade Govindan tried to ignore that sliver of humour. In which station will I find liberation again? The three-year-old girl child began to scream again—suddenly the rhythm of the rain that lay hidden in the sound of the train's wheels hit hard against a river and scattered. A rough hand and a hairy wrist pulled back from the helplessly-crying child. The unexpected shaking of the train made some room among the passengers, like wind in a paddy field. Comrade Govindan stretched His legs, vigour rising again, and tried to escape the death that surrounded Him. He shouted up and down the compartment: 'If there are any comrades here, please pay attention! I am Comrade Aayiram Kalathil Govindan. Please give me a little space to sit. I will be getting off at the next station.'

But no one seemed to have heard Him. Or they pretended not to hear. A bearded young chap who was sleeping with his head leaning on a luggage-carrier, raised his head briefly and looked disbelievingly at Him. He then murmured, 'Hey, that's not possible. This is some impostor!', and, closing his tired eyes, went back to sleep again.

DO NOT GO TO THE JUNGLE, LITTLE ONE!

Our Pallikkunnu Hill popped up in my memory when I watched two lions attack a wild bison on Animal Planet. Pallikkunnu was like a magnificent wild bison, some five or eight kilometres long, standing by the coast with its back somewhat curved inward. It is almost gone now, scooped up and devoured by earth-movers. My house is on its northern slope. From our kitchen, you can see the jungle from where the foxes dart out now and then. The home of the famous orator and critic Sukumar Azhikode is on the other side of this jungle, beyond the hill.

When I went there this time, from my own house in Thrissur, Umma was sitting on the doorstep of the kitchen facing the hill, looking very sad and thoughtful.

'What's the matter?' I asked.

My older *itha*, who was cleaning fish, put the waste under the coconut tree and said, 'Umma is crazy.'

Umma jumped up in irritation and disappeared inside the house. I followed and sat next to her.

'What's the matter? Tell me.'

Umma stared piteously into the dense darkness of the lush wilderness spread on the hillside.

She said, 'What am I to say? Gone, all gone. The coop is all that's left.'

'So, the fox took her, just say that!' I laughed. 'Actually, that's not so bad. She shits inside the house all the time. Has anyone managed to sit on the floor and have a meal in peace? Now this house is going to be a bit more neat and clean!'

Umma threw me a fiery look.

'Oh, you're so full of yourself now, but weren't you shitting all over here back then? How many times have you soaked up the sheets, pissing on them!'

I smiled. 'Really, Umma? You really think that it's the same as a hen's droppings?'

Umma turned her eyes helplessly towards the dark forests on the belly of the hill. 'What must the fox be doing to my poor Amina now?'

Just to tease her, I said: 'That nameless fox must have married Umma's Amina!'

She flared up. 'All you've done in your life is eat eggs, so how are you even to know, you *hamkke*!'

'Umma, you can actually buy an egg from a shop for two rupees,' I assured her.

'No, an egg is not just two rupees,' she declared.

'Then what is it?' I asked.

Finding no words for a retort, she looked at me. She ate nothing the whole day. At night, each time she woke, she heard Amina the hen chirp in the backyard calling to her. She sighed and said aloud as though to herself, 'She was such an obedient hen. I'd told her a hundred times, don't go to the side of the forest! But the poor girl ran there frightened by the neighbour's cock when he threw himself at her, and ended right in front of the fox who was lying in wait. The poor girl screamed so loud! I am so old and weak now, how am I to run up the hill? My fate!'

I lay in bed smiling as I remembered Umma's obsession with poultry. For as long as I can remember, she has had four or five hens around her. Umma simply couldn't be without them.

Umma's secretaries, I would joke. All to be sent off to the fox, I would complain, whenever I came home.

No one could get the better of her—definitely not the fancy chaps who do door-to-door marketing of goods from multinational companies. Coats and ties, fancy packaging—nothing impressed her.

Once a salesman came to our house hawking electronic goods. Seeing him, Umma pulled her mulmul veil over her head. She was sunning her chickens. They crowded around the circle of broken rice on the floor. Umma held a coconut frond stalk in one hand to keep them there. The salesman stepped up, put his bag down, straightened his tie, and began his speech. 'Good morning, madam! I am the field executive of Latex Multinational Electronics. I am here to introduce some of our products.'

Umma spread the last handful of chicken feed on the ground and clambered to her feet. '*Alla*, kutty, do you have an isthri-box, to iron clothes?'

The young chap gave a cool, fashionable shrug like white people. 'Yes, sure! It's one of our prestigious products—the Luna ironing box!'

Umma was barely managing to catch his words. He wore braces, and so when he smiled, his teeth looked damaged. She asked, 'Ah, *alla, mone*, son, is there some rule about not cleaning your teeth when you go around selling stuff?'

The man was flustered. Umma now launched her second query.

'*Aatte*, tell me, how much does it cost?'

'Two hundred and fifty rupees,' he said, not letting go of English.

'I don't know your engleesh. I will give you thirty! You must agree!'

'Umma,' he broke into Malayalam, 'two-fifty. Company price!'

'It's people who buy stuff who set the price, not the company!'

The salesman's multinational company-stuff turned to nothing in front of her grit. He loosened up totally and broke into a laugh; Umma laughed back. In the end he said, 'I give up! You are impossible, Umma! You give me just sixty rupees.'

She handed him the money and asked, 'Son, who all do you have at home?'

'Achan and Amma passed away when I was a child. I've been in this line of work for some years now. The pay is nothing great, but I have to get by.'

'Your mangalam? You never married?'

'Married for love! She is Christian, I am a Hindu. We have a baby girl.'

'You should raise her as a Muslim!'

'Why, Umma?'

'Why? Fighting and quarrelling! You won't have to get anyone for a nice brawl! Just you three—Hindu, Christian, Muslim!'

He laughed and laughed.

'And how old is your daughter?' asked Umma.

He smiled at the memory of home. 'She will be one this Tuesday.'

He was about to leave, lugging the heavy bag on his shoulder, when she said, 'Have some tea before you go, son.' He could not refuse her affection. When he finally left, Umma gave him two rolled-up hundred-rupee notes. 'From me for your baby girl's birthday. Get her a new frock!'

He took it, and the tears flowed. '*Alla*! Stop crying over small things! It's fellows like you who make this place go *vedakku*! All weepy at things big and small! Go now, and come back one day with your wife and the baby.'

Coal-black-tongued Nabisu, our neighbour whose nickname came from the fact that whatever she praised or even just talked about was inevitably struck down, blighted, came visiting the next day, and Umma told her, 'Did you hear? About how I bought the ironing box? He said two-fifty, and I got it for sixty! I busted him! Ha! No one plays games with me!'

'Where is it? Show?'

'No, no,' Umma said, 'I won't! If you see it, you will say something or the other about it, and it will spoil!'

Whenever she got news that Coal-black-tongued Nabisa was on her way here, even if she saw barely her shadow, Umma would run around and get all her chicks under the basket.

All these are your superstitions, I would tell her.

'You say that because you know nothing! I have suffered so much at the hands of black tongues and evil eyes!' Umma would sink deep in the whirlpools of her tears. Her children who never returned. When she returned from the mortuary, Umma had cursed Coal-black-tongued Nabisa. 'How many times did I warn my boys that they should never be anywhere within her eyeshot! There's an eagle in her eye! Oh my *rabb*, strike me dead!' The boat accident in the monsoon had proved disastrous. The bodies of only two of her children had been found. The third one was still missing.

Despite this, whenever Coal-black-tongued Nabisa visited, Umma would serve her tea. But never would she show her the hen-coop.

When she left after the visit, Umma would gather all of us children, and, wrapping together some salt, dried chillies and mustard in a piece of paper like a little packet, she would draw circles with it around our heads and throw it into the hearth. Hearing the mustard popping in there, she would exclaim, 'Ooh! Just listen! How much evil in her eye!'

One day a carpet salesman called Karim came to the house. Umma chose a red-coloured mat and asked him the price.

'A hundred rupees,' he said.

'Can't it be less?'

'How much will you pay, Umma?'

'Thirty. You must make *kabool* to that!'

To her surprise, Karim sold it to her. Handing him the money, she watched him from the corner of her eye. 'You haven't robbed me, have you?'

In the middle of many *qissas*, he asked her about me—the son who wrote stories—about where I lived.

'This is his house. He's my son. But he's now in Thrissur.'

Karim couldn't believe it. 'I like his stories a lot! I adore him!'

'No one but Allah is worthy of adoration, son.'

'Don't you read your son's writing?'

'I do. But I can't understand it. Four lines, and I get sleepy!'

'Not even a little?'

'Nothing except the photo!'

'Umma, don't you feel proud when you see his photo and everything.'

'No, actually I feel sad that he ended up the way he did.'

'But why?'

'Haven't you heard—famous in town, famished at home? Photos won't get us the rice, son.'

'Don't you know his book is being taught in the colleges and all?'

'Don't know what this fellow who can't even climb up a coconut tree is going to teach all these children. May Allahuthahaala protect us from all dangers!'

Karim became a regular visitor. When I went home once, Umma was looking rather glum. My older sister, *itha*, explained. Umma had some ten or twelve chicks. Four were snatched up by the crows, two by the eagles, and the mongoose took three. And just the other day, the fox took the last one. With so many chicks gone, Umma went nuts. She went to bed that night without food and water. She kept mumbling in her sleep, to goodness knows who. This obsession with chickens made me suspect if *itha* wasn't a bit right, if Umma wasn't really a bit abnormal—just a teeny bit. Otherwise, why would she bother so much? Work so hard? There were Tamil chicken-sellers who arrived at your doorstep the moment eggs hatched in their farms. They would call out, 'Chicks from Balumuthu chettiar's farm! Three rupees for one! Sale price ten!' Umma would greedily buy those brightly-coloured chicks (each dipped in a merry deep colour!). Twenty-four hours each day she would fuss over them, keep talking to them, coddling them, giving them names. But inevitably, despite her close watch, the crows first, the mongoose next, and finally the fox, would devour them all.

One day, Umma made a secret request to Karim. Let me see, Umma, he told her. The following week, he came over with four full-grown chicks. No sooner had they hopped out of the carton than she exclaimed, '*Ayyo*, these are also machine chicks!'

'How did you know, Umma?'

'I can make out! Look at their faces—such a smug look towards all of this *duniyavu*! Poor things, they really think there's nothing they don't know. Look at them turning their necks carelessly and swiftly and leaping and strutting around! Don't have a clue where to go, of course.'

When I went there after a two-week-long trip, there was no sign of the chicks.

'Didn't I tell you? Those were machine chicks! The fox and the mongoose took them all. I heard that the chickens in your place are good. That Rosamma who eloped here with the coconut tree climber Thomas—she told me.'

I saw what she was getting at.

'All right, now I see—this is what you were up to the last time you visited me. You were visiting all the neighbours and chatting away to get some idea about the poultry around there.'

Umma looked like a child caught in the act. She had a completely different intent behind her words 'Don't I miss your children!' when she came to Thrissur for a visit.

When we were about to set out from Thrissur to return home, she said, 'I have a cardboard box. You don't worry about it, I will carry it myself all the way.'

'What's in it?'

My wife who stood behind the door suppressed a laugh as though hiding a secret.

'You must not get angry. It's a cock and a hen. Nice black native-bred fowl!'

I hit my head in despair. Plenty of luggage, and more than two hundred kilometres to go! Seeing my face redden, Umma repeated, 'You don't have to carry. I will hold it.'

This was the lady who had to be taken to the hospital two times a month for breathing difficulties. 'I swear on Allah, I am not touching the poultry box,' I said.

The bus-stop was one and a quarter kilometres away.

Guilt poked at me seeing her struggle. 'Give it to me,' I snapped, snatching it from her reluctant hands. The box shook and the fowls inside began to cackle nervously. Not knowing what to do, I stood at the bus-stop holding the box cautiously, making sure it did not shake. Umma stood beside me, surveying the countryside, as if she was seeing all of it for the first time.

When we reached the town, a town-to-town bus trundled in from somewhere. There were just two seats free in the very last row. When we squeezed ourselves into them, my mind was on the chicken carton we had placed under the seat. The bus went over a huge bump on the road just before we reached Changaramkulam, and we were nearly thrown off our seats. The fowls in the box below went crazy with fear and began to cackle loudly. The entire bus woke up and turned around to look. The town-to-town hurtled down the road at a furious pace, tossing us up at each bump. The fowls cackled in sheer fright. Each time, our fellow passengers were shaken out of their stupor and small talk, and they turned around seeking the source of the commotion. In between, one of them said, 'It's the Tamil traders—*annaachis*! What a nuisance they are becoming these days!'

I gnashed my teeth in frustration. I was going to be caught any moment. I wasn't even able to sit up straight on my seat. This was truly embarrassing.

Noticing my pique, Umma turned her head the other way, swallowing a smile and sneaking looks at me. After sometime, a seat in one of the front rows fell vacant. I gestured to Umma to get up and occupy it. She was a back-ache sufferer, after all. Umma darted forward and sat there with a mysterious smile.

Misfortune is twin-born with me—and so, very soon someone sat down on the empty seat next to mine, and my stomach lurched when I noticed that he was an acquaintance. A university student whose doctoral work was on Post-Formalist Identities in the Scene of Malayalam.

Once he joined the programme, he abandoned the smart dressing style of the tucked-in shirt and creaseless pants for a loose jubba and coarse mundu. Praying that he wouldn't recognise me, I turned my face away—for if he did, things were going to get acutely embarrassing. How nice it would have been had these blasted fowls not got in the way ... what all could we have discussed about Malayalam literature!

I told you, misfortune is my twin. So it happened. He noticed me, and exclaimed in happy surprise—Hello! I smiled sadly.

'Hope you are well,' he asked.

'Yes,' said I (if only these wretched birds hadn't ...).

'I am writing a novel.'

'Very good!'

'There is such a drought in that genre these days! And you must be writing at least thirty pages a day! Need a lot of strength, right?'

I grunted in response. Noticing that I wasn't my usual cheerful self, he asked, 'Is anything the matter? I hope you are well?'

I nodded but my eyes wandered to below the seat—the fowls! Allah in heaven, the hurdles in the path of my literary activities! After all, discussions are literary activities too!

What I had feared happened. When the bus went over the speed-breaker before Edappal, the birds screamed and cackled deafeningly. Alas, each of those bumps on the road were thumping hard on my chest.

At each shock, my friend, the research student, bent down and peered under the seat, completely clueless about the origin of the cacophony.

'Huh! These *annaachi* Tamils! A real pain! Take your eyes off them, and they are stealing and snatching! And now, lugging around fowls and birds! The guy must be sitting coolly in one of the front seats!'

But then suddenly he remembered the sad state of contemporary Malayalam literature, and so, the conversation turned in that direction.

We reached home. The two-hundred-kilometre journey had exhausted us. Relieved at being out of the bus, I asked Umma, 'Are you really crazy? Is there no poultry in these parts?'

'It was really irritating, wasn't it? Don't be angry, son. Here there are only machine chicks, my dear. Only the native breed knows the enemy at sight!'

She opened the carton and let the two birds out, stroking them lovingly. She brought down their beaks to the water bowl. They drank from it greedily.

Umma swelled with pride as she told us of her dream.

'From these two, I will hatch twenty-five chicks, who will cackle louder and louder at the hint of the fox's presence! Son, the machine chick is just pretty. The native breed isn't like that. Do you have any idea what all it teaches its chicks when it is hatching them?'

Suddenly she froze, struck by a memory. Totally out of the blue, like she had forgotten something, lost something, she burst into tears.

'Ah! My Allah, Rab-ul-ameen! I forgot to teach my children how to swim!'

THE HORSE

The horse was indeed dashing ahead.

No iron hook in the stable could hold it back. Its master raged and wept, but the poor man did not know that he was never its real owner. The horse always looked like a doleful old man. But no one knew of the doomed animal-spirit that coursed through its lonely hours of silent prayer. Its never-ending jinxes grew pointed, needle-like legs and stepped beyond its single raised hoof. The jinxes ate and drank for the horse. The horse-gram they ate and the grassy fields in which they grazed contained the fuel that fed the simmering embers within the horse. Neither the mist of the month of Makaram nor the monsoon could quench that fire. The horse's true master was this faint inner flame. The ever-multiplying arrogant commands issued by the human master, the way the horse sprang up at his mere touch, the slaps of affection upon its flesh—none of these, in truth, justified the human's mastery.

The horse was indeed dashing ahead.

It zipped on the edge of moonlight, celebrating its unfettered swiftness. Hills and mountains were overthrown under-hoof. Flimsy clouds scattered.

But each time this happened, the horse's former births let loose a drum-roll of warning. But to no avail. The horse's guilt raced along with its speed, which kicked everything out of the way.

The horse was dashing ahead.

It flew over the abysses of ice, and towards the limits of breaking dawn. It pushed past the doors of hell. Never did it lend its ear to lamentations. The horse spoke to its much-flogged spirit:

I declare this my Independence Day. From these soaring heights, I see no more highs and lows on earth; it looks flat, plain-like. The expanse of sand beneath my hooves, my humble slave. In a single leap I freed this slave of its master. Let islets that have no inner strength, that are fragile, continue to disintegrate.

No load is a load for me today. My sole burden is my organ. Let all the shackles I broke stay put in the old tales. Let the towers of time collapse.

The horse was indeed racing ahead.

The master's unending prayers and tears, and the horse's own self-reproach that clawed at it occasionally, neither feel like a burden to the horse. Yes, today the horse celebrates the speed and the self-mastery of freedom.

You haven't seen the sea that broke all bounds and lashed free deep inside. You saw only the sad serenity of the aged face. I waited for the horns that tried to wake up and sprout inside my head. The agony of my soul, silently hoarded; the aches of love in search of death; blind force that banged against iron surfaces; cowardly meekness that retreated in fear; beds of straw laid out by the tiring rhythms of recurrence that wearied me. The urine-scented nights spent on them; the throbbing of an uneasy spirit that no sleep could soothe; and in the end, after I was cheated by myself and slipped and fell headlong into sleep—look, the sunrays fall on my eyes. I am tired. Sleep, do not leave. I am tired ... The 'I'—the first person—of yesterday is dead. This is merely the dead weight of my body. I am not at all a horse. I am the fatigue of the mule which briefly showed itself in between, somewhere in my lineage. O Master, I take back all that I dreamt up. I am but frailty in the form of a horse. Master, leave me your shoes, I will carry them. It was in some fit of delirium that I tried to subvert my fate. Please pardon me, as though I were just a harmless bout of fever.

But this repentance lasts just a fleeting while. The juice of the horse-gram slides down the gullet; the west wind surges through the mane. I change when they touch me. I am not him. Not the one I spoke of. Horse. A stallion. A surging sea of spirit confined within the iron bars of the cell. It is a horse that neighs proud, raised upon my single hoof. Even the scents that collect in my nostrils are void; they are denied to me. Derisive words, offered in response to my entreaties. Who stabs the gallop in my body, who holds it down with the tip of a spear? O False Master, I am a stallion. Not just a seat for you to sit on, or a mount to travel on.

The horse rushes on.

Plateaus and mountain ranges are mere dust beneath my hooves. However much one may hide, one has no escape from the violence and the good and evil interred within. When you try to sneak off, your good and bad burrow through the earth and grab your legs. Neither training nor care will do any good. It is a wound that turns sore no matter how you cover it. It will not fail to break its inner chains and burst out in a moment of pressure.

The horse dashes on and on.

Now the horse does not hear its master's prayers and screams and curses. It is now unaware even of the weight of its body. But then, here, right in front of its dying embers, a womb, smiling joyfully! The horse sees its long-dead mother. Amma opens her womb and calls comfortingly:

Come, come, quick ... get in through the vagina!

The horse gathered its remaining strength and leapt into the bowl-like form etched on the horrendously-torn-open fleshy sky. It left its body outside and entered.

The saddle-seat hairs of the abandoned horse-form, now bereft of a master, began to rise up.

BEAST TO THE SLAUGHTER

Yesterday I bought a slaughterhouse. The effort I had to take for this was enormous. I can never forget how I went in search of the house of the owner of the abattoir and waited at his ancient doorstep for hours, breathing air that was heavy with the stench of decay. I had to go to that faraway village night after night, travelling past the hills and jungle and fields where serpents rested. I took that risk only out of the hope that he'd come home at least after nightfall. On the nights I sought him, the sky was smothered by the new moon's pitilessness. I carried just a lighted torch made of dried coconut-palm fronds. I had no companion to go with me. Those were times in which everyone had abandoned me. Even the torch I held had no interest in me; many a time, it chose to extinguish itself in the middle of unruly thickets and ditches, annoying me immensely. The rainy season was passing, and so the crickets released their needles of sound from tiny village paths, which punctured my ears. In the vast expanse of paddy fields, frogs made a racket, singing of demon and devil.

Despite these, I kept going to the abattoir-owner's house in search of him. Each time I was met by massive doors that stayed shut. Only after I knocked for a long while would a woman, probably his wife, appear. After the ancient doors creaked open, she would extend the light of a hurricane lamp into the verandah. And throw an exasperated look at me. I would be waiting there, mired in the weak light. My tongue would move very slowly, and my voice would rasp in sheer anxiety.

'Is Muthalaali not at home?'

There would be no answer.

Only muffled voices and an eerie jingle of bangles came from the other side.

My second sentence would be born into that silence.

'Heard that the abattoir at Karangad is up for sale ...'

Silence again. The vague talk and jingle of bangles that caressed it, from the other side.

'He's not in. You come at another time.'

I would stand defeated in front of the doors, now banged shut, for a few moments. Then I would drag myself back on tired legs.

I am sure that, despite this, I sought the owner of the Karangad abattoir again and again, a thousand times at least. I *will* find him someday, I was certain. The thought that he may sell it to someone else did not bother me at all. For I knew he was waiting for me in some unseen, unfamiliar place. He would not sell it to anyone but me.

You may perhaps chide me saying—Friend, so many other professions exist on this earth, why did you have to choose just this one? I have asked myself the same question many times. Do you know how long I have used this question to waylay my stubborn mind? In spite of that, I took the trouble to enter this line of work; I exerted myself to no end to buy the abattoir. I took the bus to the owner's faraway village and threw myself into the pain of this endless quest. Each time I returned worn out but with the hope that someday, *someday*, I would get to him. I'd lie down to rest on the bedsheet of my exhaustion, actually feeling relieved, but then the question would waylay me—why choose this work? Why couldn't I turn away from it?

In the end, I did get an answer. My fate. That's the lazy man's easy answer-it-all response, you'll say. An imposter's trick, you'll tease. I do not take that seriously. I have just one thing to say: this response is the most I can muster. I had to find the owner of the Karangad abattoir in order to meet my fate. I needed to buy it from him.

In the end ... finally, I found him. It was sheer coincidence. I identified him in a milling sea of people, and it felt like an astonishing revelation. Though I had no clue what he looked like, I was drawn to him magnetically. I pushed through the swirling crowd in sheer joy and went close. My eyes spoke the language of entreaty. He was at the city's outer limit. Brimming with intense hope, I asked, 'That closed abattoir in Karangad ... it is yours ... isn't it?'

He recognised me easily. A thin layer of compassion spread across his rough look. 'You are the one who comes to my house seeking me every day, aren't you?' His voice was not the least yielding.

I nodded.

He began to speak in a slightly accusatory tone. 'What sort of a person are you? I had locked up the shop for so long. Waiting for you. Just you ...'

Wrath filled his bloodshot eyes. They then grew hard as stone.

This is the background to my purchase of the abattoir. Actually, that's not an accurate account; to say that 'I bought it' would not be true. The truth is, I did not have a single coin to buy it. But he did not hesitate even for a moment to give it to me.

Handing me a blood-stained bunch of keys, he said, 'Open the shop at dawn the day after tomorrow. Before daybreak it should be full of animal limbs dripping blood. There should be a blood-drenched head with bulging eyes mounted there on a hide ...'

His words flowed endlessly. When they ended, they sounded like an irresistible command ensuing from the terrible and pitiless mouth of a cave. I turned into a pliable mind and attentive ear. I was now all for him, my mind alert.

Suddenly, he changed into the garb of purity. Then he went away, climbing into a vehicle that had appeared as if only for him and disappearing like a wondrous thing.

What all must one do before opening a butcher's shop? I had a good grasp of such things. And that is why I decided to meet the Eminent Citizen first of all. I became a humble voice in the verandah of his mansion. Tomorrow is the inauguration of the butcher shop, I let him know. He nodded.

What was the meaning of that gesture? That he'd come? Or wouldn't? I do not know. Maybe I could have used my intelligence to poke at the way he nodded and discern its real meaning, but I had no time. There were many things to take care of. The rusty locks of the slaughterhouse had to be opened and the butcher knife retrieved. I had to scrape off the blood-fungus from the solid wooden block on which the bones were splintered. The cobwebs had to be swept away. The blackened, blood-splattered walls had to be white-washed.

I finished all of this rather well, more or less, and returned on time. I had with me the butcher knives, the chopping blades, and a small axe. I stuffed them all into a big bag. On the way back, I went into the rentals shop and rented some important stuff, including a gaslight. I had to haggle somewhat, but the shopkeeper did not hesitate to give them to me.

I reached the front of the mosque with my bag full of butcher implements. Leaving the bag in a corner, I went into the hall and offered two rak'at sunnath prayers. Then I walked into the muezzin's room. He was asleep in that tiny room in an ungainly posture. I could not wait for him to wake up; there was no time. It was getting dark. Many things had to be done. The slaughter had to begin by dawn.

I had to wake him up. He groaned and stirred, clearly annoyed. Then sat up, still groaning.

I said, 'I am opening my butcher's shop tomorrow morning. Not inviting anyone for the slaughter. As the muezzin of this mosque, I am entrusting the job of telling everyone and inviting them to you.'

I climbed down the steps once he reluctantly hmm-ed a yes. Then I took my bag and went to the slaughter-shed.

The blacksmith wasn't the least bit reluctant. He sharpened the butcher knife and repaired the blades. I went to the rentals shop with the sharpened implements.

The shop was shut by then, but the shopkeeper was waiting there, impatiently, for me. He had lit the gas-lantern, and neatly laid out the other things I had rented.

All arrangements for the abattoir were now done. Luckily, I also found an assistant, a young boy. He was an orphan; he could not think on his own at all but was very obedient. I assigned him the rest of the tasks and went home.

I ascended the steps of my house feeling relieved of many burdens. Just one more task was left. I needed to be at the abattoir at the crack of dawn. My thoughts could not reach beyond this task. They wilted. They were numb.

I lay, faintly comforted by sleep. I turned the needle of wakefulness towards the moment of the journey and waited for daybreak.

The dawn is mistier than usual. Now I am walking effortlessly, as if through well-trodden paths. I can see everything. Hear it all. I can know it all.

At the end of the straight line of daybreak, there is the abattoir. Outside it, waiting for me, the gaslight's radiance gently undulating in the mist. I am getting closer to that light. My mind is becoming stormy. The fount where the emotions are distilled is breaking. My eyes are welling up.

I look at the sky. There is a star, all alone in the dark. It glows and throbs like my heart. It looks at me with compassion. I raise my hands to it and pray so loud that my heart breaks:

'Almighty God, may the claim that one loses consciousness as the knife slices through the gullet be the truth ...'

The lips of the star move. Divine words flow from them. They pour into my heart a gentle and merciful smile.

PALANQUINS THAT RUN BACKWARDS

Of course, everything happens so unexpectedly.

Before one can sit down to think or break free and run.

That's how suddenly History returned to the streets.

In their hands were cycle-chains, like long chains of prayer-beads. Bombs like balls of rice. Knives with blades as thin and fine as palm-leaf manuscripts.

The street-lamps blew up. The thirst-quenching jars of water in the roadside shelter crumbled and fell. Bunches of fire bloomed in torches. The buses, the trains, were stilled. The needles in watches froze. It was so dark, no one could know the other. Heartbroken screams all around. We turned and turned anxiously. The darkness, everywhere. A dagger was thrust suddenly, piercing the air. An iron rod smashed a head. When? How? No one could say. Rows of bullock-carts hung with lanterns passed through the street. Their bells rang like death-knells. The air was filled with fine dust that spread an ancient scent. From some unseen corner, the clock struck.

How quickly History came back to the street!

The calls to prayer fell silent halfway through. The hymns were disallowed in the middle. The headstones of the graves that Tipu had dug fell off and crashed on the ground.

Now they float in the sky. Something like glass hits the ground and shatters. There's smoke everywhere, and a terrible cacophony. Behind the screams and curses, the History seminar isn't over yet. Verbal duels. An orgy of arguments, counter-arguments, cusswords.

No brain-piercing memory bothers us now. The pain of obligation remains only where memory lives. No worry about the arrears you have to pay the grocer Govindan Nair. No running from usurer Nanu's serpent-like pursuit. No last date for paying exam fees. No tattered shirts. No bothering about the lack of milk in your tea, or ration rice that reeks of cow-dung, or hunger, or anaemia, or sobs or tears. The smoke is everywhere. The smoke of History. The smoke of Faith. Or of arson.

Now the horse-hooves are getting past the bullock-carts. The torches burn bright and die, seething. A man burning like a torch rolls on the ground. Will he escape? The street is full of corpses. They have taken over the place. Now, like the wily lizard about to catch its prey, the palanquins creep up. Palanquins borne by corpses. They are dragging inside yet another living human being. They trample underfoot the piteous cries of his mate and disappear from sight. Now another ... and yet another ... and so on and on. The street now looks like a huge palanquin. Why, History is now walking backwards hurriedly through the street where no one is left! Yes, backwards. A wilderness now sprouts on the street. The slimy algae of antediluvian ways now creep and conquer homes. They evolve into caves. Inside a cave, a newborn babe sleeps, covered with leaves. But now, a python lunges at his sweet little face, jaws wide open ... God!

A PAGE IN THE HISTORY
OF EVOLUTION

I really don't know how many times I have been on this quest.

I am sitting in this small room inside the circus tent, facing the manager, sweating profusely and passing through moments of deep anxiety. With me is someone who has followed me since the day of my birth—Fear. It is my deepest wish to be able to speak to this world, at least once, like a wild animal. It is true that the forms and nature of Fear kept changing. But in effect, they were all the same. First, a thick fat moustache, then a cane with a small-pox-scarred face, and then an accounts book with printed pages of iron ... Or, take a look for yourself—this manager, this enormous circus tent—what else can they gift me but fear? You really have to experience it to get a sense of how I got inside here, skulking and mortified, all crumpled up like an unironed cotton shirt! All this while I had locked up my animal in a dark cell, bringing it to heel, beating it black and blue. Its piteous cries and screams, demanding a reason, flowed down its blackened face and dripped from between its bleeding broken teeth ... In the end, feeling completely exhausted, I collapsed over it lovingly, got up before it did, and entered the new day. In moments of solitude, I can hear it inside the cage in my mind, grunting and growling at me. Even as I sit in this manager's office cabin inside the circus tent, in front of his shiny table, I am aware of my animal, its struggle to suppress a roar, and the sad climax of that effort.

It is true that this is a very big circus tent. But I am amazed. How neat and pretty this office is! Like a mosaic-floored room in the topmost floor of a four-storey mansion. The fan moves overhead; the phone rings on the table. The flush door closes behind you when you step out. From a corner, the busy, constant sound of a typewriter. Extension switches to different rooms, the water-jug and flower-pot. The employees who come in and go out of the room. The manager who puts his signature on many different files, beads of sweat gathering on his wide forehead and thinning hairline. The straight hair that is blown off by the breeze to reveal even more of the balding head ... Each movement—did I not say—is like in a fancy room on the top floor of a four-storey mansion ... But I am still unable to adjust to this room. It is full of the scent of horse-dung. And of the piteous cry of an elephant when the iron hook sinks into its flesh. The cloth-wall hanging behind the manager's chair that flutters mildly in the breeze—I see everything behind it. I know all of it.

I sit here in a condition worse than that of standing up. The chair is a cushioned one. I can ease myself into it and lean too. I can relax these legs which are now pulled together with a force that could break the bones. If I want I can also relax this neck which is now turned and fixed towards the manager's face. It's possible. But I can't. I have crushed underfoot the violent freedoms of my wild animal. A moment's distraction, and this creature will slip away—and that will be the end of everything. In this room, everything except me moves freely. I am waiting for my time. I have never been able to avoid the moment in which such suffocation gets the better of me. Will my dreams and hopes betray me? It is the hearsay that the manager is somebody easily moved by the pain of others that has brought me here. I have to tell him everything: Look, this is the river of fire that I have swum in, this is the hill of thorns I sink my feet on, this is the noose in which I am trapped. *Saar*, I am the unfortunate question arisen from a very large family. The heir of seven hells. Please save me, please. I beg you, I will fall at your feet.

People are coming into the room and leaving. How am I to untie the bundle of my personal sorrows and complex problems here? My friend had told me, tell him everything. You won't have to exaggerate anything, you are exaggeration itself. Tell him. He will listen. He will surely help you in this state. Just that your situation must catch his attention. That's all that is needed.

The room is in a state of flux. The fan moves. The typewriter moves. People come and go. The manager leans on the table and checks files. Behind the cloth-wall, a horse tries to break free and run away. An elephant trumpets wretchedly. A tiger roars. A lion yawns. Even the silence that enters now and then is so full of pain.

In between, the manager raised his head and looked at me.

'Um, yes, what is it?'

'*Saar* ... I ...'

A young woman, probably a trapeze artiste, enters. Her alluringly-fleshed body undulates playfully with each step, sending the eyes into a frenzy of desire. Her smile is enticing. I kick the animal once more.

She is there to see the manager.

How am I to unpack the bundle of my pathetic, ugly situation in front of her? Just think. I am also a dreamy young man. I cannot utter a word unless she leaves the room.

She is there to ask for leave to visit her home.

When she leaves, I glance quickly at both sides, press my hands down on the table, lean forward, and slowly pull my voice out of my throat.

I barely say '*Saar*' when my throat gets clogged by my misfortune. All the doors to ease and nonchalance shut tight. Where to start? Where to end? My problems stretch and change shape like a blob of phlegm dragged by an ant.

When I collect myself, a very short man, someone readily recognised as the circus clown, enters the room. He needs some cash for his wife's delivery. I think of his wife. God must have made her just for him. Whatever is not standard, whether it is the body or an idea, is a laughing-stock for people. I heard people outside debating on whether his child will be his size or taller, hooting and placing bets.

The manager gives him some money, and then gets up and pulls out a book from the shelf. The clown hasn't left yet.

The manager turns to me.

'Tell me, what's your problem?'

I'm breaking down again. The clown is looking at me. Pressing his short, bent arms on his hips, he leans to one side and stares intently at me. I am much taller than him. How can I reveal my sad state in front of him?

I keep silent till the clown leaves the room. After that, I succeed in presenting my problems to the manager. I tell him everything. Reaching the last word, I grow silent, my throat hoarse with emotion.

What my friend told me was true. The manager is indeed a very compassionate man. Otherwise, why would he spend so much time gently listening to the personal woes of another man in the middle of such a busy day? Once I finish, I look at his face sadly, feeling worn out.

The manager is lost in thought. He is thinking of a way to save me, I'm sure.

After a short while of silence, he says, 'All right. Do something. Come tomorrow morning. We will find some way.'

I reach the circus tent early the next morning. I enter the manager's room bending my head to get under the tightly-wound ropes holding up the tent, breathing the air reeking of horse-dung.

He points to the chair, gesturing to me to sit down.

His face is buried in some files. He is jotting down something rapidly. How efficiently he manages everything in this huge tent all by himself!

This time I am more relaxed. I don't lean back in the chair, but do stretch my legs out a bit.

Suddenly, I realised that the manager was not as relaxed as he was the other day. A stern expression now rested on his face. I opened my eyes to reality and pulled back my legs.

Suddenly, something breaks out at the farther end of the tent. A man runs into the office, looking terrified.

'The lion in cage number C has escaped, *saar*,' he says, panting.

The manager seems unfazed. After a brief moment, a smile moistens his lips.

'Where can he go? When he returns, don't feed him for three days. Put him in the small cage. And don't let him ever mate again. Don't relax the punishment.'

Something moves inside me. The wild animal. Its claws are beginning to show.

When the man leaves, the manager turns to my affairs. 'I feel really pained by your predicament. I was thinking about it till you came—what sort of work to offer you? Tell me.'

I am now quite flustered. How foolish I am, to never have expected a question like this!

'I examined your records. Why didn't you write the exam?'

'I'd prepared well, *saar*, I knew all the answers. Then I asked myself—if so, why did one need an exam?'

The manager raises his brow in astonishment, as if he has grasped something of what I said, and lets out an unsightly laugh, shaking his head. Then for a while, without letting go of the wise know-it-all expression, he shuts his eyes and stays silent.

He then asks again, 'Tell me, what work can you do?'

'Something that no other person here can do, *saar*.'

He laughs.

'What's that "something"? You are extraordinary! Amazing!'

I am stuck again.

The miserable wail of a dying puppy and the dreadful roar of a hungry tiger rise up behind the cloth-wall. The sound of dry palm-fronds being torn off the palm tree, and the anxious loud chirping from birds' nests. Which monkey did that horrid, cruel bit of mischief?

'I am leaving, *saar*.'

Looking helpless, the manager says to me, 'The truth is, knowing your situation, I really would like to help. I don't have any work that would suit you in this office, but didn't you mention you have something new to do here? Please tell me about it. Newness—that's the challenge before every circus company. We are with you. Tell me more?'

I grow sweaty and tired. Somehow, I manage to bid him goodbye and leave.

Like a fool, I bury my face in the answer I know. That answer has no language. It will be born only in the future. I am the near-dead human form of the word that will be born only in the coming century or after many more centuries. This is the only truth I know. Just this: *Saar*, a human who, by chance, lost his way in the wrong part of the history of evolution, was murdered and eaten by other animals. I am that human. A human who should have been born only in the future. Born in the wrong time, he was killed in just one night. And then, killed once again by newspaper reports that raved about a 'rare infant'. I am that infant that was born and that which died, *saar*.

In my sleep, the manager guffaws. Towards the end, he laughs like a beast.

I am in the circus tent again after days. I come running hearing that their show is over and they are about to seek new pastures. The very last of my hopes is dying. That is more than I can bear. The sleep of many days has put out the light in my eyes. I am ready for any kind of surrender.

I hurry here, and am met by the empty space of the maidan. The tent is dismantled. The animals are being sent away one after another. The workers are unwinding the ropes from the last pegs. The manager is in a corner, supervising them. He recognises me from afar and comes up close. His deep concern is apparent on his face.

'Why are you late, my friend?' he asks. 'I have been waiting for you all this while. I trust that you have come upon that novel suggestion for us by now?'

That is an unexpected blow. All my hopes collapse.

This man is a scientist who wants to experiment with my life-blood.

I break down, totally forgetful of my surroundings.

'I have nothing to do, *saar*. I have no language. Please let me stay in one of these cages. Please make me an animal. My teeth, bones, any organ ... please extract them as you wish, *saar* ...'

The manager pats me on the back.

'The chance of you becoming an animal has passed a long while ago, my friend. We will be back again after many years, in this very same place. By then, maybe your new idea will have found its language. Farewell!'

The last pegs have been loosened from the ground and loaded in the truck. They are waiting for the manager.

I am standing in the middle of this maidan like a solid peg, like a language that has no emotion, like an emotion bereft of language. I stand here like this,

on one leg
in the dark
in the rain
in the sun.

BODHESWARAN

Outside, a police jeep braked.

I was taking a nap.

My sister came running and shook me awake, almost wailing loudly.

'Look, the policemen are here ... Oh my Muchilott Bhagavathy, I am going to faint!'

I lay there, remembering ...

'Why are you getting so scared? This is 1995, not the Emergency.'

I pulled the lungi around my waist and stepped out. A policeman called out to me. 'Is this the house of Kaduvakodan Narayanan?'

I got it. Probably the annual day celebration of the old case. I said, 'Yes, that's me—Narayanan.'

'What work do you do?'

(Ah, I can't bear the sight of you!) 'Work that's more honourable than yours.'

My sister pinched me from behind. She was terrified.

'Ooh, dear god, will you please remember, these are policemen?'

He hadn't expected that reply from me. He was a bit rattled.

'You draw pictures?'

'Yes.'

'*Saar* is calling you.'

'*Saar* who?'

'The Circle Inspector, Bodheswaran *saar*.'

'I've just woken up from a nap. Should be okay if I just come over to the police station by myself?'

'*Saar* told us to bring you in this jeep.'

'Does it have a toilet for me to shit in?'

The Head Constable looked somewhat discomfited.

'You're making fun of us?'

'Hey, no. I am dead serious, *saar*. I need to shit, badly. Please go on ahead. I'll be there soon.'

I lit a Dinesh *beedi* and went towards the toilet.

The policemen looked at each other, sighed, and went towards the jeep.

*

I am sitting on the verandah of the police station. I have told a policeman to inform the Circle Inspector that I have arrived.

The arrival of the police jeep, four-five policemen coming to the house, summoning me to the station—all this were causing a minor earthquake in the neighbourhood. We had just some hundred and fifty rupees in the house. By now, my sister must have put it into Muchilott Bhagavathy's *hundi*. Not her fault, really. The wedding is day after tomorrow. The bride's family will die of shock if they come to know of this.

A policeman with a paunch that was in fashion way back in Sir C.P. Ramaswamy Iyer's time comes out of the Circle Inspector's room and calls aloud:

'Kaduvakodan Narayanan, the artist.'

I stood up.

A smile crept out of those whiskers, as bushy as the untouched rain forests of Silent Valley, like a rare lion-tailed macaque, mocking me.

'Your name is rather like a dried sardine! Scared me! Ah—go in, go in, *saar* is calling.'

All the courage I'd gathered up till then started to seep away. What was he going to say?

'Son-of-a-murderer' perhaps, or 'son-of-a-*****'.

I walked on that vague tightrope. No sooner had I reached his desk than Bodheswaran leapt up and clasped my hands.

'I am really sorry, Mr Narayanan, you being an artist, I should have come over there to meet you. But, the workload is so pressing ...'

I was clueless.

He pointed to the chair and asked me to sit.

Gripped by a faint fear, I looked behind me. Is the chair really there?

They had first made me sit on a chair like this during the Emergency.

I sat down on it, very carefully. In 1975, political prisoners were most actively handled by this police-chair— three-legged chaps, two-legged fellows, one-legged, some with no legs at all ... we had to sit on them first ...

Bodheswaran sounded very polite.

'Though a policeman, I am a great lover of the arts, sir.'

That quickened my fear.

He continued speaking.

'I consider painting the finest of all the arts.'

My eyes began to grow dim with fear.

'Sir, I ... long time back ... that is around 1975 ... and all ... for people in the Samaskaarika Vedi and all ... made some minor posters ... only such things ...'

But my feeble voice was drowned in Bodheswaran's pronouncements about the excessive presence of modernism in contemporary art, revivalism, Dadaism, postmodernism, Picasso, Dali, Karunakaran ...

In between, the tea and *parippuvada* arrived.

My teeth bit into four tiny stones in the *parippuvada*.

Bodheswaran smiled.

'It's from the police canteen. To get snacks from outside ...'

I finished drinking the tea. Shoved into the file on the desk an undercooked piece of the *parippuvada*. In revenge against their shoving cloth down my throat back then.

I asked, anxious, 'Why was I called, *saar*?'

'Yes, let's get down to business.'

Rummaging in the desk-drawer for something, he said, 'I am an admirer of yours. Why is it that there are no works from you these days?'

'I don't do art nowadays. Just drawing for a livelihood.'

'I heard. Portraits, right? You're famous in that line too, I know. Portrait-making is also an artistic activity, Mr Narayanan!'

The joy of having found something lit up Bodheswaran's face. There was an old photograph in his hand when it emerged from the drawer. He handed it to me and introduced it with utmost respect.

'Uppu Bhargavan Pillai—Salt Bhargavan Pillai—follower of Gandhiji. He went to make salt with him—was arrested, jailed. My grandfather.'

I looked at the photo.

The colours had faded. The face wasn't clear.

'I want a portrait of my grandfather made. I don't care about the money.'

(I do)

'You wouldn't have another photo, would you?'

Bodheswaran looked sad. 'No. Even this was recopied from a group photo.'

(That's going to be difficult, Bodheswara)

'When will the portrait be ready?'

'I'll get it done soonest.'

'What if I come in two days?'

'You can eat the wedding *sadya*!'

Bodheswaran laughed. 'Mr Narayanan is witty!'

'Not a joke, *saar*, I am getting married after two days ...'

Trying to mask the change in his expression, Bodheswaran asked, 'Really, why so late?'

'Ill health, *saar*. I had to be treated in an *enna-paathi* for two whole years. The *uzhichil* and *pizhichil* and other treatments emptied my pockets.'

'Uh-uh, what was your illness?'

'I was thrashed.'

'Really! An artist like Narayanan getting beaten? Who did it?'

I got up and tucked Bodheswaran's grandfather's photo away safely.

'All right, then,' I said, 'let me take your leave. I will come later.'

Bidding me goodbye grandly, he repeated the question: 'Who attacked you so cruelly?'

I moved towards the door, but stood there for a moment, breathless.

I could not help saying—'Assholes like you. During the Emergency.'

What was Bodheswaran's expression on the other side of the flush door that was now shut?

*

Back home, I found a large crowd. My sister was wailing loudly. I could hear her.

'*Daivame*, Good God, they took him like this once before and he'd to spend two years in the medicated oil-*paathi*! Oh my Muchilott Bhagavathy, what fate is this!'

People were trying to calm her down.

'Kalyani, don't worry, Othenan and Sankaran have gone ready to get him out on bail, if necessary. Please don't wail like this.'

When I reached, people stood up, looking worried and scared.

I said, 'No one's singing the national anthem here, please sit.'

In between, Kalyani rushed out, hugged me, and burst into tears.

'Nothing's wrong, *mole*, he called me there to commission a portrait.'

She found it hard to believe and sobbed harder.

I showed her the photo.

She stopped crying.

People gathered around to see it.

'Can't see anything, Narayana.'

I sighed. People trying to make out what was in the photo cut through the straight line of my sight.

*

The wedding had no pandal, no percussion, no ululation—just a *sadya* for some fifteen people or so. It was over with this minimal pomp.

When I tied the *tali* around Sumathi's neck, my mind was astonishingly empty. On the four walls surrounding that void, the shadows and marks of fear.

Sumathi added sugar to the milk that Kalyani had boiled, and brought it in a glass.

Our first night together. The question to Sumathi lay throbbing in my fleshly prison—did Keluvettan tell you everything? This question was eating up my insides. When I brought the glass of milk to my lips, the taste of pure sweetness hit my tongue from across twenty-four years. I started.

'Kalyani didn't tell you, Sumathi?'

'What?'

'That I can't have sweet food?'

(Kalyani must have shut her eyes to it—since it was an auspicious sweetness.)

I felt the solitude of solitude. I clasped her hands. The question I had held inside so long came out now. In a low voice, I asked, 'Did Keluvettan tell you everything, Sumathi?'

'What?'

'About how the police had taken me many years back, and I ...'

'Narayanetta, before Keluvettan told me anything, everyone knew ...'

Silence.

Sumathi said, 'And did Keluvettan tell you about me?'

I took her hand and kissed it. The scent of raw pappadam filled the kiss. 'Yes, Keluvettan told me all about you, Sumathi.'

'What all?'

'About your first marriage. And how he left you ...'

Sumathi leapt up. 'Uhh! He left me? I am the one who left him! The money I made from making pappadams from dawn to dusk ... he'd spend it all on drinking!'

She began to weep. A woman's needs, her pain, all of it he drowned in the arrack ... the devil. The electric lines in my brain broke. The sparks flew.

'So what Keluvettan said ...'

I comforted her. 'Never mind. Forget it. Don't remember anything that shouldn't be remembered. That's the only reason why Narayanan is still alive.'

Our night moved towards sleep. My eyelids refused to shut. I saw Death's noose hang above me, swaying gently in the dark. It didn't add up. The dead nerves are in the grave, Sumathi. Didn't Keluvettan tell you?

Sumathi hugged me tight in her sleep.

The barred rooms divided themselves into four. Under the walls, pathetic, agonising pain. Pain of the soul pulled apart and broken. The lips dried up and turned into stone. Water ... The water they gave to douse the thirst was salty and sour, and reeked so bad, the stink poked hard in the nose like an iron rod.

Urine, it was.

On a tilted chair, the body pressing hard on the backrest, legs split apart, taking the lathi's blows on the penis. The blood splattered around.

'Write, you ... write! Victory to the Revolution! Draw a picture of Marx.'

Red dripping on white paper. The half-death of losing consciousness. The fits.

'Water ... *amme* ...!!!'

Sumathi shook me awake, holding a glass of water.

Kalyani's eyes were red from weeping.

Where am I?

*

The policemen came three or four times.

'We're here to get the picture. Bodheswaran *saar* was asking if it's ready.'

People stopped getting scared and worried at the sight of the jeep near the house. It became a regular one. When I looked at the photo Bodheswaran had given me, for some reason, I couldn't help laughing. If the police jeep stopped in front of Narayanan years back to land him in an oil-*paathi*, now the jeep comes to find out if Bodheswaran's grandfather has been put into oil colours!

Kalyani would bring the tea.

'Whom are you smiling at, all by yourself, Narayanetta?'

'Hey, no, just remembering the thrashing in the old lockup.'

How quickly the pall of fear fell on Kalyanikkutty's face! (The things Narayanettan thinks up for a laugh!)

'Etta, have you finished the Circle Inspector's grandfather's portrait?'

I wanted to laugh again.

'Girl, I can't make anything out of that faded photo.'

Sumathi Amma will return only after a week, her younger brother came to tell us. She's got more orders for pappadams than usual.

The laughter in me fell on burning coals.

Sumathi was turning into a long-sighted memory, weighed and balanced over and over again. All that Keluvettan told me were lies. A simple young girl, he said, who didn't want to satisfy a man. That's why the first one left. Now she's growing older. You too need someone to give you a sip of warm water in the end ...

I tried to add up all the small and large amounts of cash he'd taken. Could not remember anything. His business, of trying to find me a bride, alone, seared my mind. Whenever I talked to Keluvettan about this, he'd brim over with moral outrage at her: 'Ha! What a terrible world, this! Oh, where is our world heading towards, Narayana?'

I was as still as a corpse, my tears frozen, in the nights that Sumathi spent weeping.

Suddenly, the growl of the jeep and the sound of its sudden brake were heard. Bodheswaran arrived with a soppy smile. Sounding like a foolish dandy, he began to talk aloud before he stepped into the house.

'This is the trouble with artists. They weave dreams by themselves, in solitude. Transfer them to the canvas when they can, in their own sweet time!'

I searched for a chair with a loose leg, deliberately, and brought it out for him.

'Sit.'

Kalyani made the coffee in a nervous hurry.

As he gulped the coffee down, Bodheswaran's impatient query surfaced. 'What's the progress, Narayana, on my grandfather's portrait?'

'It's just taking shape, *saar*. I am struggling to find the mood.'

'I'd wanted it in two days, now it is five whole months. I am losing patience. I am most probably going to get promoted next month. Will probably be in Thrissur. Or Ernakulam. You know, I won't be able to come here frequently.'

I discerned police language behind his words.

'Just got married. Some problems on that front. And generally, low mood.'

'This is no creative work, Narayana. Just a portrait. I am not an artist, but I do know some things about art. I feel that you are withdrawing using low mood as an excuse ...'

'Please don't misunderstand me. Next week, for sure.'

'No, take another week. I'll come myself.'

The rage of that old pounding-stick, rolled on the legs of prisoners back then during the Emergency, was seething under Bodheswaran's words. His shoes smacked the ground as he walked towards the jeep. The world turned cruel again.

*

Yesterday, Bodheswaran came again. Luckily, I had started some preliminary work. I lied to his face as soon as he walked in. 'I have some doubts about your grandfather's appearance. Otherwise it would have been done by now.'

He didn't believe it. This time he drank only half of the coffee Kalyani made him.

He said, 'Mr Narayanan, if you need more money, just tell me. How many times am I to come here burning the government's fuel? What are people going to think of me?'

Seeing him to the door, I assured him, a bit embarrassed, 'No, *saar*, I will bring it to you—to the station, or to your residence.'

He started the vehicle, but turned to look at me with a cruel laugh. 'Narayana, this isn't a joke like shoving a piece of *parippuvada* inside a file! If you can't do it, you must tell me at least the next time.'

So he had noticed it, the *parippuvada*!

Then, regaining composure, he asked, 'When should I come?'

'Tomorrow morning,' I said, flatly.

'Tomorrow morning?' He could not believe it, and so, repeated the question. 'Tomorrow morning?'

What I needed was a determined start. Then some meditation, concentration. The portrait must be delivered by tomorrow. I started drawing.

Bodheswaran's grandfather's form started emerging bit by bit from the faded photo. By the time my sister called me for dinner, the portrait was nearly done. Just a few final touches were left.

Bodheswaran is a nuisance. His presence and the khaki interfere in memories unnecessarily. They crush me.

After making a show of having had her dinner, Kalyani said, 'Heard Sumathi Amma is filing a case.'

After the feeling of being ripped apart rose and fell in my mind, the question with no answer surfaced again.

'This marriage, she thinks, was a trick to cheat her of the money she made from selling pappadams, she claims.'

Why is this towel not able to wipe off the oily remnants of dinner from my hand?

'Sankarettan had tried to mediate. She was very disrespectful to him. Etta, she called you *ayyaal*!'

'Never mind.'

'She apparently asked Sankarettan, if he just wanted someone to hug in bed, why couldn't he have just got a long pillow made?'

I steadied myself against the pillar. My eyes were rocks that held off the rushing stream of tears.

'Will Sumathi say such things?' Kalyani waited a long time for me to answer.

I went back into my room, head bowed. The solitude of the night wafted into it. Do not let the tears come. You are Narayanan—who did not cry even when they packed ice on the top of his head ...

*

I mixed the black and the white coloured oil paints with the brush, aimlessly.

Death had come crying to me so many times, like a refugee. Why did I remain? On what grounds? The smell of burned oil filled my consciousness. My nerves—that were now dead and buried in this body, their grave—were full of death's deep guilt.

The body that lay limp in the oil-*paathi*. Saliva mixed with bile. Joints burned, torched, cooked. Nerves, beaten to a pulp with the lathi. 'Write, you son of a dog, write! Victory to your fucking bitch mom's revolution! Where's the other bastard?'

George is in Thrissur now. Runs a private bank that borders on usury. Along with it, he publishes books and does DTP. The chief minister back then, Achutha Menon, had intervened—so, he has kids. George's father is rich. Kaduvakodan Narayanan's father rolled *beedis* for a living, so the lockup was tougher on him. And besides, George went to an English-medium school.

Sumathi, that Keluvettan trapped us both. That brow of words he raised to me was so hollow; I kissed them. Forgive me.

A lonely night, with just me and Bodheswaran's grandfather. Its ship is empty and it sails silently. It journeys alone, eternally.

I took a drop of the oil paint on my brush and raised it towards the grandfather's eye. It happened in a flash. Uppu Bhargavan Pillai moved gently on the canvas. He moved his lips: 'Narayana, careful, my eyes!'

My brush fell to the floor involuntarily. When I bent down to pick it up, Pillai straightened his coarse *khaddar* cap and said, 'Really, Narayana, what is all this for? I went along with Bapu, got beaten up, died. My son was a traitor, and he made it big, made money. When his son Bodheswaran plies his higher-ups with liquor and meat, he needs someone to stay on the wall, so that he can occasionally say—this is my grandfather, he was with Gandhiji ... was beaten up in the struggle for freedom ... Wipe me off, my son. Let me fly free in the boundless, invisible valley of death and forgetfulness, my child. I have done you no harm, ever.'

I raised my head. 'But what about Sumathi?'

The head with the *khaddar* cap bowed. The Gandhian who never wore slippers—I hugged his feet and wept like a child. 'Here, take my hand, *muthassa*. Please take me as well to your valley. Tomorrow, when Bodheswaran sees my dead body lying limp below the canvas, let that police cap be taken off in respect.'

Grandfather Pillai said nothing.

The form that emerged on the canvas was frozen, immobile. Only the frayed *khaddar* on that emaciated body fluttered.

*

It is dawn.

Outside, the jeep stops.

Footsteps. The shoes smack the floor.

Bodheswaran is coming.

To take Grandfather away.

BEAST

It was very late. His wife had been waiting for him; she was worn out now and had fallen into a troubled sleep. The day which had made her wrestle non-stop with numbers in the bank had exhausted her. And on top of it, the burden of her pregnancy.

He parked the scooter in the shed and switched off its headlight. He had a two-way key to the front door, which he opened and entered. Outside, the radiance of the moon was waning. The moonlight got past the glass panes of the window and lay beside her, hugging her tired face. He was ravenous. She mumbled drowsily, 'You must've had dinner?'

That moment, the machine-like existence that awaited him at home every day came to his mind: you must have had dinner. He filled his stomach with tap-water, then adjusted the mosquito net that covered their daughter's bed, and prepared to go to bed. The foam-mattress shook a little when he climbed in under the mosquito net. His wife was half asleep when she said, 'Was vomiting the whole day. Felt really sick ...'

He sat up, gazing at her. He felt an immense tenderness. Pulling out a key from somewhere in his mind, he entered the loving husband. The tattered, fading moonlight had not yet left her. Gently, he put his hand on her belly. You weren't able to see the doctor even today? He wanted to ask her that question. After wrestling with himself for a short while, he asked, 'Are you asleep?'

Just when he thought she was in deep sleep, she replied, 'Maybe because she worked for so long in the US, this doctor's very strict. Will prescribe something for the nausea only after the scanning is done. Now, the day after tomorrow, I have to go and get the ELISA test done.'

'ELISA test?'

'I asked why. There's apparently a government circular ... Just when I was thinking of taking leave from the bank ...'

He moved his lips to say something but stopped mid-way.

In truth, he was numb with shock. He heard someone scream 'no, no!' through the many subtle shades of expression her words contained.

He should have been able to laugh aloud and ask, 'ELISA test? What for?' Why was he unable to do that? He began to burn slowly from the inside.

The moonlight outside had died.

He feared darkness like a child. The dead seemed to be waiting around his lonely void.

The expressions of his own self of long ago, of his stormy youth that yearned to feed the wild wolves. Though he had cut and served himself up over and over again, the hunger remained unappeased. Its guilt-ridden greed. Not one or two ... what was the lodge he'd gone to in secret with Sivakumar, shivering in the cold? It was that nameless woman who arrived in the dead of night, looking lifeless herself, who roused him for the very first time. (Sivakumar's fever-eaten fingers were so thin ... the fleshless cold skin clung to the bone ...) The Tamil woman from Poonamallee High Road, Chempakam. And the sweeper in the Bombay hostel where he'd spent two years, Karthika—she had many men. He felt bound to his cot, like Prometheus. The dead were picking him clean.

Karthika looked even more beautiful. Like a *yakshi* ready to lure men to their deaths, she stood there with betel-leaf-reddened lips asking for some slaked lime.

Go away, go ... away!

She is clawing now at his heart.

His childhood. In that vast prison-house of memory, his eyes are always bound. That golden pot which boils over all the more when covered—it tipped over and fell many times into his emotional world that was now juddering with fear.

The disconcerting sound of the pot falling, twitching on the floor, in the long corridor of darkness.

'Who is that?'

The dead are coming again in the dark.

He tried to escape. The door was locked. He grabbed the key and tried to open the door. It didn't work. His hand shook. Look, the souls from beyond are nearly here. Dear God! Ghosts of mere skeletons that died of fever. He tried the key. It didn't fit the keyhole. It slipped out of his hand. He looked again. But this is the key! And it is a two-way key!

'What are you rummaging for in your sleep?'

Wife. Outside, it is day.

It is a cold winter morning. Yet he's been sweating.

He lay in bed pointlessly, eyes open. 'I'm going to take the afternoon off.'

She said, 'Can you come with me to the hospital? She doesn't like it that I go alone every time. In the US, the husband has to be present at each visit, it seems.'

'You said the day after tomorrow, right?' he asked, as if he was accepting a verdict.

'That was yesterday.' Wife sounded irate.

If so, what happened to yesterday? He searched in his memory. Where did he lose yesterday?

The hospital felt like a bustling supernatural world. The sea of death. Port city of travellers who arrive, return, and leave.

As the needle pierced Vimala's greenish vein, the blood broke and moved up slowly into the syringe. He felt like it was his own blood.

He was now on the verandah of a court. Someone called him from behind.

John?

John the Redbeard. He had henna-ed his beard and made it look quite repulsive. He was like this back in the days at the tuition centre too.

'What are you doing here, sir?'

He started. Pointing to Vimala, as if he was pointing towards a mistake, he said, 'Wife. Vimala.'

'What are *you* doing here?' he asked John.

'Was doing nothing after the hospital management course. Thought this would be good training. I am working here now.'

When Vimala came out, he said mechanically, 'I once taught him in the tuition centre.'

The technician arrived, and John introduced him: 'Sheiley, this is my teacher from the tuition centre!'

She took off her gloves and smiled.

(He couldn't help telling himself: God! How shapely her lips! But why aren't they mirroring in my mind!)

'The result will be in only by the twentieth. Nothing serious, just a routine government exercise.'

'Has any earlier patient ever tested …?' he wanted to ask.

He usually stood outside the temple and smoked when she went in to pray. But as usual, the wife made a try: 'Why don't you come in and pray too?'

He hesitated.

The revolutionary of the 1970s. The old firebrand that sold copies of *Comrade* and *Vaakku* to pre-degree classmates.

The other day, a former classmate who had come to renew his LIC policy had mocked—'Comrade, when is the revolution coming?' The sadist was jabbing a new iron heated on the old fire into his heart. He didn't let go despite the bland smile. 'Yes, add a new one, Jeevan Dhara. Whether LIC or Marx, it's all the same, isn't it—everything's to do with the economy!'

As he stood praying, he felt someone ask from within: Who am I?

'You sinner, you've ruined everything!' Vimala was wailing.

He lay throbbing in pain on the cross of perspiration.

'Let's kill ourselves with poison. Or go away for good …'

The night-train was hurtling on.

Vimala lay curled up on some Marathi newspaper in the space in front of the train toilet reeking of urine and beedi-smoke, their daughter looking at them piteously with sunken eyes framed by a head of dry, brittle hair.

'*Mole*, my little girl! Your *acchan*'s sins!'

Outside, a station sign-board in Marathi flashed past, like the other-world.

Writhing in her fever, Vimala wept weakly: 'You reprobate, you terrible sinner ...'

He struggled up.

Vimala was touching him gently from behind.

He groped in the dark. Is the floor of the compartment so smooth? This is a foam-bed. This is home.

Vimala said, 'Take this pill ...'

He stretched out his hand mechanically.

She held him close now. 'Didn't I tell you to wipe yourself dry and rub the *rasnadi* powder when you came in soaked from that drizzle the day before yesterday? Did you care to listen? And see, what's happened? Fever and delirium!'

'Where's our daughter?' He pulled the words out of his throat.

'She's in the other room. Didn't want you disturbed. The Regional Officer called last night. To inquire about your health.'

'Wasn't my life over, torn to bits in some decaying periphery of the town?' he asked himself silently as he held Vimala close and sobbed.

Someone came and drew the curtains back. It was day outside. He mumbled amidst his tears: 'God, please don't forsake me. One chance. Just one more.'

'This is the fever talking,' said Vimala. 'Lie down.'

For the first time in his life, he realised that pillows could be really comfortable.

'The whole of last night you were snapping at some TTR in Hindi, saying he tried to kick you out of a train, or something ... What happened to you?'

He held her close. 'Won't you forgive me?'

Not comprehending, she merely looked at him.

O Maker of the Other World where Truth and Untruth remain unmixed, take back the mighty oceans of memory. You remain in me like the invisible limits of pure water that dissolves in the salty sea. Your Truth, produced by disease and cure together, is imbued with the logic of Great Reality, incomprehensible to me. Give me at least a drop of your limitless compassion ...

John smiled, caressing his dirty red beard.

'What?'

'The change in you, *mashe*. The sandalwood mark on your forehead.'

He quickly wiped it off. But then, that very moment, he also felt that he should not have done that.

John stopped smiling and called the technician with the blood report. Every inch of his body seemed to be riddled with thorns.

Sheila smiled. 'The ELISA result will be ready only the day after tomorrow. The other results are okay. Just reduce salt in your food, that's it.'

John kept talking in the middle of the silent drum-beats of conflicting feelings. The technician, Sheila, glanced briefly at him, smiling warmly. He woke up. She walked away, her shapely buttocks swaying. He could see nothing but pieces of bum-flesh stuck on a skeleton while John was asking him something about life insurance policies.

That night too, he rode on fever-trains. In his delirious slumber, he passed by unknown north Indian slums, the bright clothing of people there, wheat, potatoes, onion ... The TTR threw him out of the train: You dog, you feckless wastrel ...

Mol jumps awake and cries. She is in a charity home, in a queue for the sick, for rotis and potatoes. Someone snatches her food and she weeps loudly, helplessly. Mother Teresa picks her up and gives her a kiss. His eyes grow moist. How quickly was life snatched away! On its other side, when a sinful life ends in fever, the curse ... You sinner, terrible sinner!

The Regional Officer was smiling. 'Take good rest.'

The clear stream of the real world. Vimala.

'This is a seasonal fever. Here's the tablet.'

John, can you please speed up the damned test result that's killing me slowly?

Sheila is on the intercom.

He secretly eyed John. What was he telling Sheila in that corner?

Are hospital employees sneaking looks at him? Why did that light-eyed girl at the reception point him out to her colleague?

'Hey *mashe*, what's that sneaky look on your face? Worrying too much?' Saying so, he smiled. 'Was just passing by, and thought I'd ask.'

Then he called out to the technician again. 'Sheil-ey, is *mash*'s result in?'

The phone rings. It is not loud, but how sharp the sound! Sheila.

The cover is opened.

Negative.

All the windows that were shut are now open.

Thank you, God!

Sheila smiled genially.

For the first time, he found John's henna-stained beard attractive.

Sheila asked something about a suspended LIC policy. He explained it with unusual and unnecessary eloquence. John put the test result safely back into the cover. Sheila said goodbye.

Stepping out into the corridor from John's room, he found it impossible to stop himself from turning around and staring at Sheila making her way back to the lab.

THE SON OF JOSEPH

On a night untouched by even a solitary star, I was invited to the feast. My life was that of a complete outcast. The messenger let me know that the food would be prepared specially for me.

That pitch-dark night was reminiscent of life at the unfathomable depths of the murky sea. In between, some things took human form, saluted, and disappeared as tiny flashes like radium needles. I was exhausted from hunger, of body and soul.

I asked that stranger, 'Friend, where is the feast going to be held?'

'I've been entrusted only with the task of delivering the invitation,' said he. 'I don't know anything more.' Like an extinguished lamp, he disappeared in the darkness.

I loved life greatly. When shoved out of eating places, I got back in through love. I took revenge on those who stripped me naked by putting on the raiment of dreams. When they blew out the lamps, I rekindled them with reverie. But the eyes of my soul were still filled with darkness.

Why does a human being stay alive in the world? To be stoned by fellow humans, to fall senseless from it? To turn mad from his mate's callous neglect? To see the little ones it raised run away and hide behind their mothers?

The life of all human beings is an unending elongation of gloom. The lamps and lights that appear in between make it all the more blinding. I tried to read the invitation that I received in these lights that come and go erratically—and failed.

I then wandered aimlessly in the streets of the city where lights never go out. The light there is freezing cold, like a block of ice. I was worn out fully with hunger, anger, and helplessness. I would smell myself now and then. Where is the stink coming from? Is it these clothes which I have been wearing since many days now, or is it my soul?

In the end, I did find the feasting hall to where I had been invited.

At its entrance hung a large board with the sign, 'Welcome to the Abode of God'.

But the security guards would not let me in. Instead of throwing me out physically, they used words and logic to bind me. They reminded me of shrewd lawyers. Their arguments were flawless. But the justice in them served only to pierce the palms with sharp-tipped spears of iron. There was no compassion in them. There is nothing as hostile to humans in this world as justice without mercy. They kept firing their arrogant queries at me:

'Who are you?'

'Where do you come from?'

'Who invited you?'

'What? You couldn't see his face clearly?'

'What's the evidence?'

I was stunned, stupefied, like a villager trapped before a haughty government official.

I was staggering from hunger and the cold. My sunken, bloodshot, yellow-rimmed eyes must have terrified them. My filthy clothes must have disgusted them. I tried to talk to them in my failing voice. Losing his patience, one of them finally said:

'Wait for a while outside.'

His voice had a faint touch of godly concern when he said that; it filled me with hope.

Many people in luxurious cars, clad in costly garments and wearing expensive perfumes, swept in and out of the feasting hall with gay abandon. Some of them were greeted specially by the guards. How magnificent these garments— they exclaimed to them. Qualities that they did not have were ascribed liberally to them. Even their tiny abilities were blown up with effusive praise. The guards behaved as though the very world had been created for these people.

I took solace.

When the whole world is hurtling that way, why should one single person stand against the flow? In a society where lies and shortcuts are the marks of intelligence, he will only appear wild and loathsome—this victim of Time.

Suddenly, more guests began to arrive.

Everyone pushed and shoved each other to enter the hall. When each declared himself supreme and they all began to force their way in, the guards were stumped.

One of them could not suppress his rage. He gathered up all his strength and gave me a mighty push!

The weakling that I am, I was thrown some distance away by that unexpected and undeserved act.

I landed in a deep canal of dirty water.

Sinking in the horrid stink that clawed deep into the brain, I began to lose consciousness.

The gloom was appearing again. In the colour of mud.

The angels sneaked in through it with their flower-like smiles. A wingless man accompanied them.

They scooped me out of the stinking water, took me away, and took care of me. They bathed me in scented oils.

While they were wiping me dry with divine cotton towels, the angels turned to the wingless man. I heard them tease him with mischievous smiles: 'Joseph, can't you see ... your son ... even now?'

YAKSHISCARS

It was the white man, Alwin *sayipp*, who relocated the Madampi Town Railway Station from near the expansive Madampi river to the vicinity of Chirakkunnu.

Behind the new railway station lay the large maidan, surrounded by a forest of banyan trees. If you looked at it on moonlit nights from the top of the hill of Chirakkunnu, the maidan in the middle and the trees around it looked like a rare, exquisite flower. To its sides were drinking-water pavilions for thirsty travellers and buckets for animals to drink from. For the ever-jingling bells that hung from the travelling bullock-carts, the maidan was a rest-stop during the day. At night, such was its desolation that even beggars and vagabonds hesitated to sleep there. But the godowns and shops near the river would be live till daybreak. The ghazals and qawwalis wafting from the gramophone in the Welcome Hotel near the petrol bunk would fill the town with music. Young men who guarded the godowns stayed awake all night on black tea and *kalathappam*. The town of Madampi—literally, 'Tyrant Town'—was shrouded with its old tales. The tiny government huts in the slums would be overflowing with music from the harmonium and the tabla.

Yet the maidan behind the railway station was cut off like an island at nighttime. That desolation was finally ended by a woman. Kuttyassan-kka remembers that she arrived there on one of the night-trains at some obscure hour on a full-moon night.

Her skin glowed like the sandalwood flower and was as fragrant. Her raven tresses fell below her waist and bore the scent of frankincense. Her laugh was like the jingle of glass bangles falling in a heap. She swung up and down the maidan's banyan trees. When day broke, she would be gone. On every moonlit night, she would come freshly bathed and adorned. For the young men there, she was both the laden table and the delectable morsel. Muscles firmed through the daily combat with timber-logs, hands calloused from lifting them—all wandered like little lambs through her vales of pleasure. The maidan stirred awake. She pleasured more than one young man at the same time. Her kisses under the canopies of the banyan trees through which the moonlight filtered—they were simply unforgettable.

'No woman could match the pleasure she gave,' said Kuttyassan-kka. 'She held men down with bliss. Sometimes the carnival of lust lasted till daybreak. She could become many beautiful women at once; the night danced past like a conjurer's trick ... But come dawn, the girl would disappear!'

'She would flee on one of the morning trains. Yes, that must have been it ...' he added.

She never came to the Madampi Town station during the day; only on moonlit nights. The well-built young men of the town eagerly waited for her to come. Swept away by the pleasure she offered, they revelled in it; their cries of ecstasy sounded like screams.

But pleasure is always in the territory of evil.

A mystery stood hidden between her and the town. Young men began to disappear. Newer and newer young men arrived, so no one asked about the disappearing youths or youthfulness. The newer ones were thirsty, impatient for moonlit nights. Their heavy sighs grew longer and finally burned and fell as ashes in the maidan behind the railway station.

When she appeared, a mere dot on the horizon, the men would hurry there. She would smile and say, 'The train was late today. Were you bored? ... Come, let's go.'

It was on one such radiant full-moon night that the young man named Kuttyassan, strong as darkness itself, fell at her feet in tears. 'I can't forget you, woman,' he said. 'My wife and son killed themselves, jumping into a well, because of this thing between us. See, still, since how many days have I been waiting for you here, behind this railway station! I'll lose my mind. I'll ...'

She did not let him complete the entreaty; she drowned the sentence in a long kiss of love. With a single step of the carnal dance, she put out the searing coals of his memory. She, and the Present, alone, danced with gay abandon on those ashes. After their third round of mating, he sobbed: 'You must be mine, mine alone. I will marry you.'

She burst out laughing. 'Lust should not be so selfish, Kuttyassan-kka! Look, there are so many waiting for my kisses and the magical pleasure I give.'

Many banyan leaves yellowed and fell on the breast of the Madampi maidan. In their place, new shoots and fresh green leaves sprouted. Fresh waves of moonlight came and went. She arrived on the night-train; Madampi maidan came alive with the warm breath of youth. On one such night when the crowd gathered, a young man called Umbaayi rolled his tea-seller's cart there. It was just an experiment, but he ended up selling a lot.

Umbaayi began to buy provisions for snacks each time the night promised to be a luminous one. Today, four or five kilos of banana. Or two hundred shellfish. Or three hundred round-*puttu* pieces, or fifteen bottles of milk ... The moonlight and the sales both grew brighter in Umbaayi's tea-*makkaani*. A lot of newcomers came—men who sipped black coffee and strong black tea once the night was over. Easy sale. Just that one had to put up with sundry groaning and moaning ... But who was this old man with shrunken legs, dragging himself along? Who was he cursing so loudly? 'She's Yakshi Paaru ... My sons, don't go near her. My son fell into the water, my daughter fell into the well and died. She'll kill your younger brothers ... she's a *yakshi*!'

The man dragged himself there every moonlit night, God knows from where. No one paid him any attention. Some threw him a few coins out of pity. That only made him more furious; he would start raving. 'Hey you, son of a bitch,' he would shout. 'Neither I nor Paaru need your coins. We are different, she and I. The oil at the Koolaath shrine is on fire ... Bhadrakaali-of-the-pyre has spirited away the sprouts of pox ... oh my children, do not go!'

He would collapse after a while. Umbaayi would hand him a glass of tea. The old man's sunken, rheumy eyes would turn towards Umbaayi.

'Drink it up, Uppappa,' Umbaayi would say, 'you've been talking so long.'

He'd begin to weep.

'Drink, please drink, this is me telling you,' Umbaayi would comfort him.

His tears would still be flowing as he slurped down the tea.

Gradually, he and Umbaayi became like granddad and grandson. And so, once Umbaayi asked him, 'Uppappa, why do you holler so much?'

'Because this granddad of yours has no one of his own, son.'

'But will hollering like this bring you any dear ones? Now, look at me. I too have no one. Just an arthritic old Umma.'

Umbaayi handed him a banana fritter. Kuttyassan took it; then, suddenly, flung it away. 'This is a *mayyath*, a dead body! The corpse of a banana! It's covered with a shroud of flour ... My son, my Kunhibibaathu was ...' He began to weep and wail. 'They were all finished by the *yakshi*, Paaru. My son, my daughter, me ...'

Umbaayi laughed. 'But you didn't die, Uppappa!'

'Umbaayi, to become a *mayyath*, you don't have to die!'

Umbaayi was baffled.

'Oh you who died by *neeyat*

At what price, a *mayyath*?

Living as a *mayyath*

Is in this *duniya* the *neeyat*

Is in this *duniya* the *neeyat* ...'

'Uppappa, is this the only song you can sing?' Umbaayi said, laughing.

'My son Umbaayi, you are a naive one, you won't understand.'

His eyes fell on the Madampi Town station. The rhythmic screech of the one-eyed goods train that passed through it silenced them for a long time.

*

Once when he was blowing into the glass lantern to revive the flame, Umbaayi told the old man, 'Looks like the moonlight will be late tonight. The local train will come at ten.'

The old man tried to clamber up, as if he sensed some evil omen. 'Umbaayi, son, you shouldn't hang around here for too long.'

'That's why I've fixed this cart on four wheels! I can go to the riverside if I want. Or to Chirakkunnu. My mother has the three of us, her children. I have to sell, no matter where—be it the holy *nerccha*-place, or the moonlight's space. That's it.'

'But this business under the banyan tree is especially dangerous.'

Umbaayi stopped blowing into the lantern for a moment.

'Have you seen that *yakshi*?' asked the old man.

'No,' said Umbaayi.

'Lucky! Don't ever see her.'

'Uppappa, tell me, why do you hate that woman so much?' He saw the wrath grow on Uppappa's face.

'She's a blood-sucking ghoul, a real *yakshi*! Sucking the blood from these young fellows—that's what she does! The chaps she uses grow weak and useless before their time ... so many have been paralysed waist down, so many have died trying to get themselves cured in the healer's oil-*paathi* ...'

Umbaayi heard that terrible story for the first time that evening. His belief bounced between what he heard now and hearsay. He picked up a glass, washed it idly, and placed it mouth down. He then began to rub the soot off the samovar. And yet he heard the laughter, which sounded like glass bangles falling in a heap, from the shade of the banyan tree. Whenever his eyes wandered there, Uppappa banged his staff down nastily. 'Don't look!'

Umbaayi jumped.

'Your job is to sell tea. If you let that laughter reach your ears, your bedridden umma will lose her son ... be warned,' the old man said.

Then, the harshness in his tone would subside. His words to himself, wet with tears, would follow, like an add-on. 'A glass of black tea, in between, when I tire, shivering from the cold ...'

'What's your name, Uppappa?'

The old man smiled without feeling. 'Ever heard of Mooppan Kuttyassan?'

'But of course! The Kuttyassan-kka who lifted Alwin *sayipp*'s jeep with his bare hands! *The* Mooppan Kuttyassan-kka whose muscles were wrought from the dark night!'

'What you see before you is the *mayyath* of that Kuttyassan-kka, son.'

Umbaayi reeled in shock.

Uppappa's song pushed its way in at the wrong time; it snorted:

'Oh you who died by *neeyat*
At what price, a *mayyath*?
Living as a *mayyath*
Is in this *duniya* a *neeyat*
Is in this *duniya* a *neeyat* ...'

Kuttyassan-kka's bitter laughter landed in a corner where the moonlight fell and broke into pieces.

That night, Umbaayi closed his tea-*makkani* earlier than usual. Later in the night, he woke up rudely from a nightmare in which the legs of the men of whole generations shrivelled in an oil-*paathi*.

*

The story is ending now ...

Many, many steam engines whistled past the town of Madampi. The maidan behind the station and the trees there were bathed in moonlight on many more nights. The beautiful woman got many more men into the oil-*paathi*. All of them were stowed away in the storehouse of secrets. The moonlight-belle and magic sex alone stayed as eternal truths. Umbaayi's tea-shop and Kuttyassan travelled one more length of time.

Kuttyassan's song and curses aimed at Paaru as well as his endless passion for her became the cart's constant companions. His piteous plea—'do not let that laugh get into your ears'—played out like an overfamiliar, therefore meaningless, song. One day, Umbaayi said, 'Uppappa, please keep an eye on the cart. I need to pee', and walked away.

Uppappa began to mumble, suspicious of the darkness into which Umbaayi had disappeared. He kept banging his staff on the ground.

The next night, Umbaayi said, 'Uppappa, don't know what it is, but there's a cramp in my tummy. I'll need to shit.'

When the flame in the lantern was nearly dead, Umbaayi returned, panting. His face bore all the strain of wrestling with a dilemma. Kuttyassan swore at him. But Umbaayi continued to give him tea. His love was unconditional.

After some months, it did happen indeed. Umbaayi complained, 'Don't know why—I can't stand for long these days. My legs are so tired.'

'Umbaayi, shine the lantern here,' said the old man. He saw it in the light of the lantern. The muscles on Umbaayi's youthful legs had shrunk. Scabs had begun to form on them. Thin legs with rough skin, like tamarind-tree twigs. Hands on his chest, Mooppan Kuttyassan howled in despair. 'Hell! What calamity has befallen you, son! Oh my Umbaayi, why did you do this to me? Paaru has killed you too ...!' He cried so hard that his throat split and bled.

*

Umbaayi's tea-cart lay orphaned. Mooppan Kuttyassan's wait tapered into sighs and tears. Umbaayi's family and the tea-cart were bereaved. Umbaayi must be lying in an oil-*paathi* and remembering Uppappa. He must be shivering once more in the greed for the bliss that Paaru gave him. He must be writhing in the oil-*paathi* with the desperate force of a vulture without wings.

The moonlight was reborn many times on the maidan in Madampi. On one of those nights, to a slave who was about to embrace her, Paaru asked the question—what is that over there, creeping towards here through the dark like a murky crocodile?

As they watched, a human form reached up to the swing hung with jasmine garlands. She looked at him.

'Paaru, do you know me?'

Paaru let out a sprightly laugh, like a quick, graceful dance-step.

'Oh, isn't this Kuttyassan-kka?'

He glowered. 'Not one man whose blood you sucked has come back!'

She ran her fingers gently through his hair.

'These hips bore the weight of Alwin *sayipp*'s jeep!' But saying so, the old man took in her fragrance and forgot everything; it was as if his lost youth had returned. He tried to raise himself up, his heart filled with tenderness.

She laughed again. 'Don't overdo it! You don't have it in you anymore.'

'Tell me the truth. Are you a *yakshi* or a whore?' He was panting with rage.

She laughed freely.

That's nature's doing. The fruit of karma.

Suddenly he remembered Umbaayi. Suddenly he became a doting grandfather. 'You killed my Umbaayi too!' In a single lunge, his hand reached her throat. His hands clamped around it.

Paaru's slender neck was in the grip of the gnarled hands that had once lifted Alwin *sayipp*'s jeep. Her slaves-in-love tried to pull him away. But how could they wrestle down the force of darkness in Mooppan Kuttyassan's hands?

In the end, they attacked him with stones and wooden stumps as though he were a coiled python. The night became a cruel dance of kicks and blows. They tore off Kuttyassan's body parts one by one. But his right hand could not be wrenched off. It held Paaru's throat with a force mustered from the very essence of a whole life.

A goods train arrived in the wee hours and passed them by, screeching rhythmically.

When the morning came, there were two corpses in the middle of the maidan. A right hand, torn off the body, cold, stiff, tightly clamped around Paaru's neck. A tongue bitten right through by her dying scream and death itself.

That day, for the first time, the subjects of Tyrant Town realised—Paaru was the *yakshi* who travelled through time. Her body was covered with pale scars and contagion. Her *yakshi*-ness and the pallor of her scars were hidden under the tiny tassels of moonlight. She looked fairer. More beautiful.

This story is ending.
The *yakshi* let us keep
its body alone,
and went away.
Time says:
Yakshi-as-woman is now deathless;
A force that rides atop the whole of the universe.
Beyond Madampi's domains,
far above the earth,
she awaits
the new nightly luminescence.

HOUSES, TOO, ARE ALIVE

What can I say to excuse myself when you ask me to tell you about a house that I once had? If I tell you that around my house were three rivers full of inner streams and swirling whirlpools, and those are my childhood, adolescence and youth, in that order, that might sound shrouded in poetic obscurity. But it is not possible to avoid rivers in this story; without talking about the rivers, without crossing them, it will be impossible to reach home.

The first river is the colour of rank cruelty. Want, hunger, bickering parents, fights, kicks, fainting, quarrelling with the neighbours. How many tender limbs of my childhood were torn off by the crocodiles that swam in it, do you know? Often, my fingers. Sometimes, legs, pulled off in a single swipe. Sometimes, my brain, in a swoop. Scared and more scared, I forgot how to cry. I stuffed the soil from the hill behind our house in coconut shells and made pretend *puttu*-cakes. I put them in my mouth and learned the difference between daydreams and the taste of the earth. Those were times when even the shit by the wayside made me salivate. I cursed God many times for not making shit edible.

The second river is mostly a deep, poisonous blue. *Puthusakthi, Geetha* and *Stunt,* all three were in love with me. They were pornographic magazines. I felt their letters kiss me; their soft fingers ran all over my body. The letters in these pages picked up this person who no one in this world wanted, took him to their secret lair, and caressed him from head to toe with feather-light lips. But they would also occasionally turn into man-eating crocodiles. Sometimes they would puncture a hole in my neck before diving into the river and disappearing. Later they would come back, beg forgiveness, and tickle my body to cheer me up. Once upon a time there was a woman called Ammini. She was a sensual siren with heavy breasts and rounded thighs. Overflowing with lust, she would pull men close and suck them dry. In those days, I used to be assailed by two doubts: first, was it true that one drop of semen was equivalent to sixty drops of blood? Secondly, did women get erect?

... And so one day, when I was sitting by the river and telling some story, words leapt at me as a gory-eyed crocodile, bit off my right arm, and escaped into the water. As I stood rooted to the spot, totally stunned, there assembled an unruly mob like a thousand crocodiles with cruel, bloodshot eyes ... I hid in the den of my wound. I lived there equally fearful of God and Devil. Hiding and fearful, my childhood and adolescence split my chest asunder, passing over it like a soot-covered steam engine.

Now, the river of youth. By this time, *Puthusakthi, Geetha* and *Stunt,* all three were out of circulation. Instead, my youth stood up on its iron feet, and stepped into the noon-show in cinemas, in which the noon-sun thrust a chisel into my eyes and turned them around. The blue 'piece' that may surface in between the endless, foolish old Tamil movies!

The impoverished youthfulness of the villages, waiting with bated breath, counting their heartbeats as the feeling boiled over and melted into shivers. The disgusting power games of dark and emaciated youth blowing *beedi* smoke on the breasts of a misshapen, low-level whore; the grunts and moans in the theatre. When the movie was over, outside, the soil on which Che Guevera and Naxalbadi had poured down was completely parched. The dried-up tears and courage of a generation. Neither friend, nor God—you did not save anything for me! Except the blindness of this ignorance. This river is full of shadows. It is in the murky waters that crocodiles lurk. The river began to steal all of my fetid, bloody memories. It is the English-fail pre-degree generation that sent the impoverished of the villages to the gallows collectively. After the upma and the worms and the green chillies of the free school lunch, you encountered English, the crocodile, in the pre-degree class. After the frantic memorising and the assertive sentences, the ones who were desperate to live would resolve to somehow swim to the shore. It was the English-medium students who filled the galleries, hooting and laughing at the sight of this struggle. Their bow-tie-clad cheerfulness was full of the sweet arrogance from Ooty, Kodaikanal and other high-flying schools ... There's a lot to say, but let us cross this river too. Come this way, we are near the house.

Inside, the burnt aluminium cooking pot with a charred neediness stuck in it. Four kitchens in one house. Beside the dried-up well, quarrels over drinking water (even the sound of pots and pans in the house are packed with so many layers of meaning!). And blood from broken foreheads. Collective wailing. Curses and frenzied words. Shaking in fear, I swim across the rivers and take refuge in childhood's gaping hole around which flesh has fallen apart. There, emotion, which has no language, falls on me like an iron bowl; it covers, shields me. When children sleep, God comes in secret to kiss and caress them, to weep over them—this is your share, drink the bitter cup, my child, there is no other way; Time needs your tears and blood in order for it to move ahead.

The house was partitioned after much fighting, cursing, and bawling with hands slapping the head in frustration. The world is full of emotions. Life is like the mustard seeds popping in hot oil. Neither the setting sun nor the moonlight knows how to communicate. Not even a bit. They are dumb witnesses to terrible cruelty. The torrents of tears that my mother wept would form a stream, seek God out, and question Him. Umma would say, 'All this is the handiwork of wayward djinns and shaitans, my son. Umbaayikka's word is rock-solid. His eyes see deep inside. Let's have a *kuth-rathib* done.' Umbaayikka's holy brass-leaves were buried at all four boundaries of the house. The lanky, lean ascetic mumbled in his half-conscious state: 'Leave! Leave! You don't know Umbaayi ... You play with me, *I'll* make you play. I will. Move out. Leave!' My older brother, given to lunacy, said, 'Umbaayikka, this has nothing to do with the djinns or the *kaali* or *kooli*. This is an American conspiracy. Just the other day, when I was sleeping, the Pentagon crept in and took away my blood in a syringe!'

Umbaayikka stared at Ikka, let out a long hmmm, and said, 'Ambu Mestiri, who hung himself from the bathroom ceiling forty years ago, has gotten into this fellow's body! We must get a good amulet written. His madness will go away.'

Umma said, 'In the old days, we would not step out of the house after *maghrib*. Soon after dusk would begin the procession of the devils and their offspring. Kooli, Ottamulachi, Theechamundi, Thondurutti, Pottappothiyan ... Kooli would emit a terrible squeal ... the wax in your ears would squirt out in bubbles. And the foxes howling, on top of it all. We'd close the doors and stay inside, scared to death. Then, shortly after four, you'd hear a horse's hooves clattering. That was the saint—the *aulia* interred in the Fakhir Makhaam tomb—making his way towards Mecca for the *subahi* prayer. The hooves would be heard, and in no time, the devils would all disappear in fright. Just the sight of the *aulia*'s head would send them scampering!'

'Can't we go pray to him at the Makhaam, Umma?' I would ask.

'No, son, we are lowborns. We can't bar his way. We don't deserve it either. Uppappa made the mistake—he heard the horse's hooves and leaned out through the window to look. A face as bright as the sun, on a white horse, clad in a red turban and green shirt. Uppappa looked just once. He never uttered a word after that, till the day he died. Uppappa's peek had angered the saint. This house was reduced to a shambles. The rice cooked here lost its vitality. You put one *ser* of rice grains into the pot, you'd get only half a *ser* of cooked rice. People started hating each other ... There was nothing but want, all the time. Was there a time in which madness and illness weren't present here?

'It's all the work of the shaitans and their offspring.'

Saying this again and again, Umma was pushing at life, making it move along slowly, as though it were a massive rock. The Pentagon came regularly to suck Ikka's blood. I got stuck between reality and tall tales, not able to tell them apart. In truth, in our time, our house was itself a ghoul. A blood-sucking ghoul. One day I saw it with my own eyes. When I was dozing once, leaning against the wall of the house, I woke up rudely to a grotesque sight. Pointed fingers had emerged from the walls of the house; they were sucking out the blood from my relatives who were asleep inside. I pulled myself away from the wall in fright.

The next day, Umma said, 'Something is dripping from the roof on my arm—take a look.'

Blood, blood for sure. Clotted, slightly darkened blood.

Oh, some dead creature on the tiles.

I wanted to tell her—Umma, that's not a dead creature's blood; that blood is of living people. The house is burping out the blood it drew from all of us yesterday.

My younger brother asked, 'I'd put all this on the table yesterday. Who threw them on the floor?'

Another person said, 'The shirt was on the hanger, but now it is on the floor!'

My littlest brother fell off the bed one night as though someone had shoved him.

Another day, Umma said, 'Can't leave a single thing in the kitchen—the thieving cat knocks it all down!'

I knew it—the house was heaving and shifting. Not the thieving cat, Umma.

Around this time, my older brother Majid disappeared. My mother went to old man Umbaayikka trying to find him. She wept.

Umbaayi said, 'He'll come back. His lunacy will be gone. He's in a dargah in north India.'

Umma said again one day, '*Mone*, blood is falling from the roof again. We must get Gopalan to clean it.'

I hid again in the fleshly hole of fear. Umma, no. It is dangerous. The house is centred upon itself. All we can do is give blood to live. In the end, small bits of bone began to fall with the blood. Umma was now really frightened. I cried. Ikka, my older brother left. For good.

Sleepless nights of blinding darkness. I sat inside them observing it all keenly. At night, the walls breathed calmly. Inside them, thousands of fiery cat-eyes wandered freely. Noses, ears, limbs, all walked about, separated from each other. In between, the eyes would bulge and stare; the ears would stop and listen closely. Something would tumble in the kitchen. My younger brother's shirt would fall off the hanger. The valuable things he placed on the table would be knocked down to the floor. The blood would drip from between the tiles. Did someone struggle, feeling hands clamp their mouth?

In the morning, my younger brother was missing.

Umma wept.

The *siddhan* Umbaayikka comforted her: 'He will come back. Probably with his older brother.'

Umma decided to hire Gopalan to repair the house. He assessed it naively: 'It's a real mess. The tiles are all broken. They should be removed to clean the rafters.'

Umma counted out her savings and told Gopalan, 'You can start moving the tiles, Gopala. There are many dead creatures lying there.'

Gopalan came on a Sunday to remove the tiles. I stopped him. 'No, Gopala, this is too dangerous.'

Umma wiped her tears. 'Oh my *rabb*, this boy's fate is the same as his brother's! What did I do to deserve this, my Rahman?'

Gopalan went up on the roof. I stepped out of the house in fear. But when the first tile was removed, Gopalan fainted. When he came to, he told Umma, 'Ummityaare, it is full of blood! Like it was collected up there! Those aren't tiles, those are layers of flesh! When I took them apart, I saw my face in the pool of blood in there!'

We were sleepless that night. Fear gnawed at us all. Umma struggled to hold her tears back.

The locals said, 'Shouldn't have removed the tiles. This is common in our houses too. Act as if you've never seen what you saw, never heard what you heard (or else eat poison and die!).

Umma spat out angrily: 'No! Never! We won't die of poison! My children and I will sleep on shop verandahs. We will tear this house down.'

Umma's words, once spoken, are never taken back.

Her golden *alukaths* and the broken gold ornaments in her box were sold to Velayudhan *sraap,* the money-changer. We decided to get really capable *khalasis*—known for their inimitable strength and skill—to break the house down.

Many tried to dissuade us. 'Ummityaare, this is another way of downing poison! If you feel so sad, why not get a TV? It'll relieve you. Goodness, so many serials these days!'

Umma didn't heed any of it. We gathered courage and started breaking down the house under Gopalan's leadership. The *khalasis* had to swim through channels of blood. The tiles came off the rafters of the roof like flesh from bone. We were not wrong. The house stirred like a red-coloured, mad elephant. It trumpeted, clearly undeterred by the centuries through which it had aged. The *khalasis* too were unfazed. They surrounded it with spears and crowbars. They attacked it, not letting it escape. The bones broke and fell from the roof. The house paused in confusion, like a deer among lions. The *khalasis* plunged their spears into its left breast; the blood flowed in channels. But what were those eyes moving among the ancient, fallen, broken mud-bricks? Infants. Foetuses. Under each mud-brick, three or four of them. Their pale and sickly faces resembled our ancestors. The bloodless infants formed a huge question mark as they stared at us fixedly. They, of course, had not learned to bawl, even.

How can I get away from there, swim across all the four rivers, and reach a place of refuge?

A HOSPITAL VISIT

'Despite everything, I believe in human beings,' he told Vimala.

Tucking twenty-five rupees in notes under Ahmad's pillow, which was reeking of medicine, he said, as though nothing had happened, 'You shouldn't have gotten into that inane fight.'

Ahmad smiled even though the bluish bruise on his eyelid was smarting badly. 'Vasuvetta, what are you saying? I had gone there to calm things down!' The vexation and pain clouded Ahmad's face as he spoke. He tried to make things lighter.

'But you are the prime accused ...' said Vasu.

That worked. Ahmad began to laugh slowly, unbrokenly.

He told Vimala again, 'I still believe in human beings. A whole caravan might arrive finally in their brains, of facts, of truth. At least a last busful of them.'

But the high tower of comfort and faith inside him was beginning to crumble. The truth is that some strange pandemic has overtaken all of humanity. He saw that Ramunni, who was occupying the next bed, was pouring Bapputty some tea. He wanted to ask Ramunni, 'Didn't you break his head with a stick in the riot?' But he didn't ask; he suppressed the question in a mild and genteel smile.

Basically, our young people are much more peaceable than their earlier counterparts. No new springtimes of idealism bloom in their paths. Young people need to be inspired, need to have a dream. That is their reservoir of energy. But if it is nudged even lightly by bestiality, the reservoir of energy is breached, and it rushes over its own blood, assuming the form of cruelty.

The occupant of the next bed was a total stranger. His bandaged legs hung over the edge of the cot.

Vasu asked him, 'Do you need anything, tea or something ...?'

The stranger replied with a question: 'Will they build a mosque there?'

His anger got the better of him. It rose up and galloped over his gentle manner. The price of ration rice has gone up by sixty whole paise, you donkey! That rose up in his mind, but when he actually spoke, he edited out the last part. He ended up panting. For a moment, he saw the jungles spreading all over and human beings in tree-bark garments eating raw meat. Really—the fear of a modern man born in the Stone Age sent chills down his spine.

Night.

When they were about to go to bed, rather unusually, Vimala told him, 'I am afraid to switch the lights off.'

He wanted to tell her, 'I have faith in human beings. Someday, the light of minds conscious of facts and truths will fall upon their ignorance. A group of travellers will surely arrive. They will come. At least on the last bus.'

THE HOLES THAT THE EARTH BEGOT

One

In the ancestral home of Kuzhipparambu—'Yard-of-Holes'—was born a baby boy, a little Unni, after much prayer and waiting. His parents spent each moment watching his limbs grow, with a happy anxiety, counting every moment. That's when they noticed. The baby boy was very fond of digging holes.

'Okay, that's what he likes, let him play, dig, grow up,' they said.

They also saw that as he grew bigger, so did the holes he dug. He dug holes in wakefulness and sleep. In the leaf-plate, when he ate. In his dreams, as he slept. He dug seen spaces and those unseen. And so they grew: he and his holes. In the front-yard of the ancestral home, his baby-holes dimpled and bloomed as he grew up.

Two

It was the social studies teacher in Class III who taught Unni that the earth is round. How unfortunate! The earth's spherical nature, when it was impressed on his consciousness, somehow included the sky as well. The subject he ended up learning in college was also geography. Each time the earth appeared on the classroom blackboard in round form, the sky also appeared to him as its better half. Why don't we fall off the face of the earth when it tilts in space? Gravitational attraction, that's it. But he wasn't redeemed by any attraction. And besides, each time he thought about it, he'd be gripped by pure terror, like that of falling down from the top of the Eiffel Tower. He made it clear: the roundness of the earth must take shape only along with the sky: 'I don't want the globe without the sky'. It became a reason for him to beat up his geography professor.

When he stepped out of college, he had in his hands a new earth. Earth-and-Sky. The sky filled with blooming dreams; the earth stirring and dancing in the spring. He hugged that earth to his chest, and slept seeing the stars.

Three

By the time it became evident that this was summer, many years had passed. He lay in the desert of reality, face up. All his stars died out in the heavy, searing sighs that blew from his chest through his windpipe. When he opened his eyes, he saw the red-hot sky. A bowl of fire covered it. The earth had blackened to its roots. He walked alone. Then he noticed there are no flat plains on the earth—only highs and lows. The earth itself is an abyss. Holes within holes within holes. The deeper he went, the more they were, holes connected like links of a chain and with hooks in them. He screamed in that bottomless and eternal darkness. His screams stumbled and fell in each and every hole, staggering aimless, orphaned. Seeing the feathered caps of the topmost holes shake their heads and laugh, he raised his head from the dark and began to count them. The more he counted, the brighter the golden light of the feathers in the caps shone. His screams had been extinguished into a silence, helplessness, and this became a painful fissure in his mind. The rainwater of tears collected in it. Then, it dried up; after all it was summer.

He told every hole that it was a hole. 'Look, the sky is a cavity; the earth is one too. When they join together, the earthly globe is formed. None of you are a match for him.'

'Match for who?' the holes asked.

He was eager to reply. But even the answer collapsed halfway through and was reborn as a question.

Four

He who did not graze in the maidans. He who did not swim in the pond. His thought and fancy were, after all, holes. This got him into trouble, you know. A girl who was mesmerised by the pretty circle of his hole laid a trap on the road, digging a hole and concealing it with the twigs of love talk, the sharp-tipped leaves of the corners of her eyes, and the supple green branches of mischievous laughter. That's how he fell into the trap. He fell like a sack into the hole. The truth is that he was really irritated. She stood by the trap-hole and laughed and laughed. Laughed so much that the plains were now all holes. His serious demeanour was now punctured. He laughed too. Now there were two laughs.

Five

That's how he and she started a joint hole. With this, the holes began to grow diverse. Many types of holes were found. She told him of holes he never knew of. He made her holes she had not known. Dimples all soft with laughter and honey, square-shaped voids, round and half-round hollows, some like the moon, some like stars ... Though they made many, only three of them stayed: one boy-hole and two girl-holes.

Six

Now the craters were almost as big as him, and frighteningly big. Their hungry, all-devouring jaws opened before him heartlessly. In the middle somewhere, his view of the earth had fallen away.

Now he realised, the earth wasn't spherical. It was a depression. It was a depression in a frying-pan, a large one. The oil was boiling in it. Below and above, the sun was burning as the kindling. He was in this frying-pan, getting puffed and cooked. Thrashing about in it, he screamed and yelled. But how to escape? The more he tried, the more he fell into the oily hole. Tiring. Tiring. Fried and burnt.

Seven

He lives now in a room shaped like a hole, where the pain of obligation towards the hungry holes does not bother him. He can close his eyes in the peace of old age. He can run his fingers idly through the grey hair of his consciousness. He can pass the time killing the white bugs in that hair.

But Time is a yawning hole too. The morning sun shows him a spider web. The noon sun pokes awake the snake of heat. The dusk fills his vague and anxious holes with darkness.

The night-hole is unbearable. In his dreams, he sees a large hole in the sand. He falls into it like a tiny ant. Below him, the death-rattle-laugh of the ant-lions. When their bloody teeth sink into his breast, when he wakes again, half-dead, yet another hole. The day. When he closes his eyes, another hole. Night. Two bottomless pits.

The holes are his iron rods. He tried to rise up above the earth, mounting on the three times of the past, present and the future, and count the holes on his fingers: one, two, three … God, how many more pits!

Eight

The holes are pain. Pure agony. Dug straight out of hell. Are they not a trap that someone wrought in the illusion of false pleasure, in the circle of beauty and bliss? O world of hellish beauty, how many more, your holes?

Can't. Not anymore.

There were a few more hours before dawn. He shook and patted down his dreams and walked unsteadily towards reality. He was tired, but his eyes were focussed. His eyeball mirrored a nook of peace. I shouldn't be a burden to anyone. I shouldn't be a burden to anyone …

In the end, he found it. A rectangular hole. He paused by its side for a moment to catch his breath. He didn't want to turn around and take a look. There is no more past. No more the past, present, or future. No seasons. The hole, only the hole. He hugged it in exhaustion and lay hugging it. The hole began to move. It began to rock like a cradle. A nipple that tasted like the earth filled his lips. The soft strains of a lullaby flowed through the earth's unseen pores and grew faint. The holes in him shut their eyes for long.

The void was filling up.

His depressions turned into false flat land. Then they smiled colourlessly. Their echoes, alone, blew as the wind in verdant forests.

PRISONERS OF THE TAJ MAHAL

Both the children were unwell. They had cried all night and finally fallen asleep sometime close to daybreak, when the electricity went off. Outside that room stuffed with humid heat, it drizzled lightly. In the end, when Shahjahan opened the window, a soft breeze and fresh moonlight entered. Someone is singing from the banks of the river, he thought. Maybe the mosquitoes?

He turned to look at Mumtaz as if he'd recollected something. She was fast asleep, worn out, with her breast half exposed. The younger child had still not let go of the nipple of the other breast.

The moonlight lacked the radiance of earlier times—it was pale and wan. Nothing spectacular, just some light from the moon. As Shahjahan gazed at Mumtaz, a terrible guilt rose up and shrouded him. She was an innocent, trusting girl, who had given up everything to be with him.

The expression on her sleeping face was a repetition of a look that was now permanently on her face. 'You'd promised that our honeymoon would be at the Taj Mahal. It's been ten years since. The Taj is for us still a picture on the page of the calendar. Shouldn't we have the means? ... Oh really! They're holding the State Conference of Persons with Means at the Taj Mahal! Just say, that our old love is gone.'

And so it turned out. When they had got down at the wrong station, the one just before Agra, she had thrown a look at him that reminded him of his responsibility. On the journey, he had asked many people for essential information—the closest hotel, the route, the cheapest transport, and so on. By the time they alighted on that unfamiliar station, the children were both exhausted. The moment they entered the hotel room, they flung away the suitcases and flopped on the bed. Oh, what a trip! At each station they had passed on that terribly tiresome journey, he had told himself—need not have started out at all. Mumtaz's never-ending whining and stubbornness was the reason. You should fly on journeys such as these. But the ticket charges for the family would probably exceed my yearly income.

The children wouldn't allow Mumtaz to recover. They cried obstinately. Each one wanted her to pick it up. Mumtaz lashed out at Shahjahan: 'Just hold one of the two and get out! I have had enough!'

The children, however, pushed him away. Mumtaz was livid: 'You are really a smart one, you know! You never cuddle them so that they won't come to you. You've freed yourself of the bother!'

Shahjahan tried to be sympathetic. 'Mumtaz, don't say that the children are a bother. They are God's blessings.'

She could not reply to that.

In truth, those words were his revenge. Watching her fall silent, he revelled silently like a lawyer who'd won a long-winded debate. Sometimes a deep desire for vengeance would overtake him, like the remainder of some malice.

'We could have brought my sister too, to help you.'

She pretended not to hear that.

After a brief interval of silence, he continued, like a victor advancing to clinch his victory. 'But you didn't agree to that at all.'

She glowered at him and was about to hit back with hurtful words when the doorbell rang and the room-boy appeared. He said something in Hindi. Shahjahan did not understand, so he looked at Mumtaz. Why don't you talk to him, he gestured—the meaning of that was: let there be some use for that Hindi MA of yours, at least this way.

Mumtaz spoke with the room-boy in broken Hindi. The truth is that neither of them could make out what the other was saying. In the end, Shahjahan managed it with a combination of broken English and cracked Hindi. The room-boy had asked what they wanted for dinner.

'I want *bathura* and chicken masala,' she said.

Shahjahan said, 'Let's stick with vegetarian food? Better to avoid meat away from home.'

She was silent; clearly, she disliked his suggestion.

He managed to order chappatis, dal, and milk for the children, half-talking, half-gesticulating.

He said, 'The dumb fellow probably understood nothing. Goodness knows what he's going to bring. What else to do but suffer!'

Then he turned to Mumtaz, biting down his derision, and remarked, 'You may have passed your Hindi MA with first class, but my twelve marks in Class Ten have served us better!'

That seared her. 'There's not one Hindi, actually there are many,' she too bit down her anger and replied.

'But I am learning for the first time that there is something like Useless Hindi!'

The child began to cry for her breast. Unable to send a suitable missile in response, Mumtaz broke into sobs. Then she said, 'But then, I didn't crawl through SSLC with pass marks. I was ranked fourth in the district. I didn't study in between loading the firewood on bullock-carts, my Uppa sent me to a respectable school.'

To avoid a quarrel, Shahjahan picked up a towel and made his way to the bathroom, feeling foolish. When the cold water fell on his head, a question came into his mind and barred the way. Why do you argue so much? Why do quarrels overtake us despite the best efforts?

Back from the bath, he saw that the waiter had brought the food. *Bathura* and chicken masala! Exasperated at not knowing what to tell the waiter, he looked at Mumtaz. She was chuckling. He wanted to join her but simply couldn't. The pleasant ripples of that laugh stayed till the children fell asleep that night. Shahjahan held her close affectionately. He asked, 'Why do we quarrel all the time?'

She returned the embrace and replied, 'I too am thinking the same.'

'What is happening to us?'

'You're really troubled by my nature, aren't you?' She began to weep.

He comforted her. 'Don't say that! It's my nature that's causing all the trouble. My peculiar way of finding fault with everything ... Anyway, let's forget all that. Tomorrow is going to be a good day. We will see the Taj Mahal you talk about all the time.'

She sighed, remembering something again.

'Oh, the years that feel so short, but are actually endless! The truth is that I'm not as excited as I used to be back then, before we got married, about seeing the Taj Mahal.'

Suddenly, the older child woke up, and began to moan and grunt. She leapt up, went to him, and began to gently pat him back to sleep. He let out a wheezy sound—bronchitis. She touched him—fever too.

'Oh God, the fever is bad! Let's forget the Taj Mahal—all I want is to get back home!'

He thought of her ever-changing nature and it angered him. 'Children falling ill is natural. We've travelled a long way. I told you that we should come by ourselves, let them stay with their grandmothers, but you wouldn't agree!'

'What to do now? My son hasn't had a cheekful of water, even.'

'Never mind. You give him a Calpol. That should bring the fever down.'

'Ayyo, I forgot to bring any.'

Shahjahan's voice now grew loud and harsh. 'I told you a hundred times to pack the medicine box! Don't you have any sense? You are always poking your nose into things that don't matter, but you can't remember the important stuff? Why can't you give me at least a bit of peace ...?'

She did not respond. Only hugged the child close.

He got up, went through the door to the balcony, and pulled it shut with a bang. Then stood in the balcony for a while, looking out. He felt the city flow towards him like a river in spate, bearing on its current the many kinds of light reflecting from tall and narrow buildings, the local Hindi-tinged bustle and nostalgic songs in Mukesh's voice, all bobbing and floating.

What was this journey for? Who was it for? ... Who is sobbing and weeping? Who is beating their head on iron railings? ... A tediously repetitive sympathy filled him now. He opened the door of the balcony and stepped in.

Luckily, the children were better by morning. They woke up feeling bright and chirpy.

The route to the Taj Mahal, the modes of transport available, the cheaper trips—Shahjahan had gathered detailed information on each. When Mumtaz began to insist on taking a taxi there, he told her, 'We won't have the money to go back home. Even now our budget is strained because we got off at the wrong station.'

Mumtaz found that easy-on-the-pocket trip, which required changing bus after bus, very demanding. The children began to bawl in the crowded buses. Mumtaz offloaded all her anger on them. It's only because we didn't get a taxi—her mind kept saying that again and again. He has the money—this is deliberate, she believed.

In the end, they arrived at the Taj Mahal in a horse-tonga. At first sight, the Taj Mahal did not impress him. Its real beauty is in the calendar, isn't that true, Mumtaz? He suppressed that question. The four of them posed for a picture, the kind you get then and there. He haggled with the photographer quite a bit over the price.

The children, however, were thrilled. They gazed at the massive dome in wonder, through eyes still drowsy. As they walked towards it through the garden, Mumtaz said, 'The marble's faded.'

'But this is truly a marvel, isn't it?' Shahjahan asked.

Suddenly she stopped, pressing her hand on her stomach.

'What happened?'

'Oh, nothing.'

He explained, 'Not just the Taj, but also the garden around it and the museum are wonderful.'

She pressed her hand on her stomach again. 'I need to go to the toilet. Didn't manage to go properly this morning.'

He reined in his rising anger and said, 'Didn't I tell you not to gulp down all that chicken from goodness knows what kind of kitchen? Didn't I warn a hundred times? How then are we to control these children?'

Suddenly, she asked a question that sounded like a slap.

'What will you do with these children if I die? Will you bury them along with my corpse?'

He was silenced.

A few glum moments passed between them.

The Taj Mahal's marble facade seemed to fade and yellow even as he was looking at it. In the end, they managed to find the toilet. In a corner behind the museum. Leaving behind the Taj, the abode of Love, the river Yamuna, the gardens, and the rather vulgar museum where historical objects were displayed in an orderly fashion, Mumtaz raced towards it.

But the door was locked.

And she noticed that many people had queued up, waiting their turn. She too waited, desperate. The children began to cry in irritation. The Taj and the gardens were lost to them. They were searching for it.

Seeing her stand desperate and helpless in that queue, a deep wave of sympathy rose within Shahjahan. As the children wailed stubbornly, his sympathy broke the laws of place and time and peeped at itself mirrored in the Yamuna.

On the way back, she sobbed and sobbed. 'What was this trip for? What did we see? Nothing.'

He held her close, gently. 'Never mind. We will come another time.'

They got a bus from the outer gate of the Taj Mahal. A ghazal that entered it by mistake played on and on. Though he did not know the language, someone deep inside his heart translated it thus:

'The world is a great wonder. Even a blossom, a garden, even a tiny grain of sand. But there is something in us that prevents us from enjoying these marvels. Someone has rolled a huge rock, blocking our eyes. O poet, sing of the untainted Yamuna. O Fingers that play on the sarangi, comfort us ...'

Though the train rocked them, singing a lullaby like a mother, he alone lay sleepless in the dark. He said to no one in particular, 'Shouldn't have seen the Taj Mahal. Should have saved at least that sight.'

ALL ALONE IN THIS RAILWAY STATION

One

There was once a railway station in the middle of nowhere. It was as if it were on an alien planet. It exhaled the barrenness of the desert and the hot winds of loneliness. Rainclouds and the rare birds that chanced to be near, flew over it with only trepidation in their hearts. The rail tracks that passed through the station began from some mysterious place and ran towards another equally enigmatic destination. Most of the time, they were red-hot; like some venomous snake in a mound of coal, they slumbered. When the wind shook the telephone lines overhead, the barrenness and isolation of this station would blend into a death-like buzz.

The station-master was a young man grown old before his time. The station had been built under British rule. The architecture, with its wrought-iron pillars and ancient ceiling, made it resemble a house of the dead.

The station-master, trapped in that great ocean of loneliness, kept writing letters to his superiors:

Respected sir,
I am not sure how many times I have already petitioned you. I am also forgetful of the years I have served in this empty

station. In fact, by now, I have lost most of my past even. So many times have I seen the leaves fall in the wintry breeze. Sir, is it not true that I was assigned this post actually as a solitary life-sentence? Can you please not cover up that truth from me, at least? When someone is kept in isolation for long, when his thoughts end up revolving around himself all the time, he is subject to social exile; he sinks into the bottomless swamp of forgetfulness. I am now sinking in it; nearly half of my body has disappeared in the swamp. The cruel truth is that this is my past. The other half still not sunk is surely my future, what else could it be? These meaningless tracks, running in front of my distraught days and nights, caught in the middle of my past and future. Dashing into the far distance on them, odd trains, whose sounds are too fast to follow. I sometimes even feel, sir, what is the point of my waving the green flag? Please, can you let me know if anyone is paying heed to this green signal? ...

He would lose concentration after reaching this far. *Is it a horn that sounds in the distance? A train? A passenger train? Or a goods train?*

Like love that could not be exchanged, the loneliness stifled him. The only link he had with the real world was Shappatti, a servant who was nearly human in form. Not sure upto what extent he can be described as 'servant', though. Whenever the station-master was hungry, Shappatti would arrive with the same repetitive rhymes and rhythms condensed into a meal. His bodily organs were repulsive. In his eyes, clannish hatred bred and multiplied. And he reminded one of the fly that buzzed eagerly around faeces. The station-master depended on him to send all his letters to the authorities by registered post. Shappatti also brought the station-master a fixed sum every month, apparently his salary.

The station-master suspected that the newspapers Shappatti brought him were false. He would ask him each time:

'You have registered the letter, haven't you?'

'Can't you meet the authorities at least once and tell them about me?'

'Did you send them a petition asking for a substitute station-master at least for one day?'

Shappatti would listen casually to all these questions. Like he were the mediator between Man and Devil. Many a time, his indifference and inattention made the station-master lose his cool:

'Where is your mind? I am talking to *you*, did you notice? Are you passing on my letters and complaints to the authorities?'

Shappatti would cast his empty eyes on the station-master. That look, repeated over so many hundreds of years, would make the station-master struggle to quell his terrible grief.

'I'll throw away this duty and leave. You think I can't do that?'

Shappatti would stand still, like eyes without eyeballs.

That scene was repeated one more time that morning. The station-master noticed that he was more agitated than usual, and that his breathlessness was a sign of aging.

He knew that a certain goodness in him was slowly corroding him, like a punishment that could not be avoided.

And that he had just one service to perform in this station. Which was to make sure that no accidents happened because of him, that two trains didn't run on the same track. Babies should not scream in sheer helplessness. There should be no mothers who had lost their babies; no widows. He heard the clang of the fetters of lifelong confinement. *Can I not step out of this station?* Suddenly, a totally unexpected train rushed past, fast as lightning, and it made his soul recoil. *Who am I? The satisfaction of well-performed duty? Or the very human form of meaninglessness?* This thought hunted him for hours after the passing of every train.

In the end, he wrote letters to his superiors again. His agony made him forget even the official language of communication. He tried to control himself so that his words did not descend into a doleful lament.

In one of these petitions, he wrote:

Why do telephone lines pass by here, sir? Who drew them so tight? The upstart of a superior official who did not bother to communicate even once?

He could never muster the courage to leave the premises of the station. That wasn't accurate really—he did go, once. Fixing his ears to the resonance of the tracks, he had walked some distance on them. That was on a really misty morning.

By the wayside, he saw demon-like telephone posts. The birds were fleeing from the single tree there as though they were frightened of something.

Each step beyond the station felt like a dereliction of duty. His heart beat harder and harder as it sank helplessly into a harsh sense of sin in which duty and authority commingled. The misty shrouded unseen distances. Had a tiny grain of sound fallen off the tracks that ran endlessly? *Is a train coming? God, my orphaned station!* He ran back in dread, picked up the green flag, and stood ready to wave it.

Shappatti came many times. He never washed his ghoulish face. The station-master filled his loneliness by stuffing his room with full-length mirrors and luxuries. He pasted the picture of a large gathering on his wall in the effort to overcome his solitude. In the beginning when he felt bored, he would look at himself in the mirror and make all sorts of funny faces. Then, when that bored him, he began to dance in front of it. He pretended that the dancer was someone else and that he was just a spectator. In time, this absurdity too lost its novelty.

Very soon, he flung away the pretty things. He began to feel the silent presence of a corpse in every object of consumption. Again, that station with its ancient reek, the unending wait for a train, the solitude, and the hot winds, hunted him.

Two

In the past years, not a single train had passed by without him noticing. Not a single train had passed without his green signal. Now, he was old. But still sending petitions to the authorities. Now, the date of his appointment, the examinations he had passed, and even the trainings he had attended, were all buried in the cemetery of his memories.

Things were thus, when one day after the winter had passed, it struck the station-master: there must be others like him, at the two end-points of these tracks. Yes! Maybe if he walked steadily in one direction on the tracks long enough, he would meet one of them. But he couldn't leave the station! *What if some train passes through it in the meanwhile? An irresponsible officer is like a moving carcass. An obvious criminal.*

Suddenly, he had an idea:

A hundred thousand trains had passed this way through the forgetfulness of the years. But not once had he seen a driver. Not one person had greeted him. The trains would pass by, during the day and night, like demon-carriages. They never returned an acknowledgment of his existence. Therefore, he made a stuffed doll clad in his uniform. It stood a little bent towards the tracks, holding out the green flag. He hid this ruse from Shappatti. *That fellow is the spy of some underworld power.*

When he saw that everything was ready, the station-master began to walk. Each step fell on the earth like a huge weight. The wind blew over the telephone lines strung tightly between poles on which the demons dwelled. For the first time, their murmur did not scare him. As he went further and further away from the station, he felt that he was being reborn on a new earth. The birds did not fly away from the lone tree for once. They looked at him like they would at a kind stranger.

To the station-master, his station now seemed only like a tiny dot far, far away. He thought that the deserted land beside the tracks was beginning to gain some colour. He realised that the ancient stink of the station that he bore on his body was beginning to fade. Did a bird sing in the distance? Did a fragrant breeze kiss him?

As he walked ahead, he knew that the journey was starting to acquire rhythm and pleasure. The mystery shrouded as distance began to dissipate.

But then, here, the tracks split. The station-master was stunned: *the tracks split and carry on by themselves. They become single tracks and run into the expanse. God, if so, what were my trains and a whole lifetime of witnessing?*

He could not stop his tears at all.

HISTORY-AS-MAYA

It's true that I have a PhD, but when I worked in the Gulf, for a long time I was a camel-herder. Since there was nothing much to do in the sweltering heat of the desert, I used to pull out my thesis now and then and read it to the camels. The first job I got was that of a goatherd. Later I chose camels, as more intelligent creatures. But what was the use? They paid no attention to my thesis. Initially I thought that the problem was their lack of knowledge of Malayalam, but soon I figured out that the real problem was the lack of loneliness. The camels are not alone. There are many things they can talk about; they can make love; they can quarrel with each other. I then began to talk to the solitary trees in the desert. Then I learned: trees are so much better than men and animals. They listen carefully to you. Sometimes they wave to cheer you on, pretending to be bending in the wind. No point blaming the camels. They are the lucky ones. They have to suffer loneliness only when they are alone; never that which comes in the middle of a crowd. If you don't mind eccentric thoughts, you'd see— the newest of worlds deal with the sale and purchase of human loneliness. When you feel all alone and bored, just step into a big shopping mall in town. You'll be suddenly surrounded by friends of all sorts. Camels and goats don't have shopping malls precisely because they aren't lonely. Failing to discover the language of the camels, I cancelled my visa and returned home.

By then job prospects down here had become even dimmer. I was weighed down by heavy debt. At home, we sat down and looked at each other blankly. It was then that a very dear friend approached me. With a job. He got to the matter very quickly: 'Don't you remember John sir who taught us physics in Class Ten?'

'He's in the US, isn't he?'

'Yes, the same. His father is here. Geevarughese *mash*.'

'Isn't he with his son in Las Vegas?'

'Yes, he was, but the terrible weather and the loneliness there was too much for him, and so he's back. He'll be here for some time.'

'Oh, he must be over eighty then?'

'Yes, but he is very healthy. As supple and fresh as a healthy long string-bean and glowing like a ripe tomato! And his memory is really excellent ... He wants someone to chat with in the house, during the day. He lives alone.'

Then, lowering his voice and throwing a quick glance around, he whispered into my ear: 'He's agreed to pay six thousand a month, plus all expenses. He has nothing else to do. He doesn't smoke. Doesn't drink hard liquor. No hanky-panky business. Drinks just wine, only the finest brands—he keeps sipping them.'

He flashed a smile at my sunburnt face. 'You'll get some too. This sunburn will disappear and you'll become ruddy and healthy in no time!'

'But then, me, who has a doctorate ... to go to a house and ...'

My friend was irritated. 'You didn't mind herding goats in the desert ... learn to live at least now. This is not a goat but a very knowledgeable, mature, experienced man—with so many good qualities combined in him. And if you make the right moves, he may even take you with him to the USA.'

Me, in the US, with my PhD on 'The Crises of the Self in the Malayalam Novel'!

But on the third day, I succumbed to the temptation and knelt before Geevarughese *mash*. He looked a lot like our Krishnamoorthy. Tall, with a fair, handsome face. True, he looked above eighty, and true, he did deploy brief silences between his words, but it was indeed a pleasure to be in conversation with him.

My friend introduced us to each other. 'This is Geevarughese *mash*. A man who lived his youth amidst major political and cultural shifts. You two should speak,' he said, bidding goodbye.

I looked at the calendar behind Geevarughese *mash*'s easy chair. It was the first of November—Kerala Day.

He spoke in a very courteous way. 'I heard you are in the Middle East. My cousin's wife's brother is based there. A very nice person. Incredibly knowledgeable about the fine arts. He had gone there on deputation from the US, to work in the oil fields. He's an engineer.'

I prayed to God. My work began. Outside, the announcements of a political campaign could be heard.

'It is a good omen,' he said. 'This is how a job should start.

'See, if I am not mistaken, it was the 1940s. I had landed up in a meeting organised by the great leftist intellectual and educationist Joseph Mundassery in Thiruvananthapuram. By chance. The local Circle Inspector did not grant the organisers permission, and it became a big issue. You must have not been born then. The twelfth edition of Changampuzha's fabulous pastoral elegy, *Ramanan*, the most popular book of those times, had just been printed in the Mangalodayam Press; they had not even unpacked the bundles. And C.J. Thomas, that revolutionary mind! Oh!'

Some retired army officers have the tendency to brag. But don't mistake Geevarughese *mash* for one of them. He twisted open easily the cap of a large bottle of ruby-red wine he had brought from the USA, and threw me a smile. 'I am still young!' Then, he poured it into a special wineglass and raised it to his lips ceremoniously.

In the interval, I asked him. '*Mashe*, where did you study and teach ...?'

'I did my BA Honours at the Madras Presidency College. Once, Panamballi Govinda Menon—leading Congressman, if you remember—came there. It was a big event—the whole place was festooned with flags, so many speeches, unending applause ... Another event was when the nationalist poet Vallathol visited the campus—just think, in those days he was huge in our minds! Whenever a car-horn sounded, we students would rush out of class to see ... M. Govindan, the radical thinker, was then living a quiet life in Madras. But there were no intellectuals who did not interact with him. O.V. Vijayan, the great fiction writer, and M.N. Vijayan, the noted critic, were both students in that college at the time.

M.N. was a very shy person, but even back then he had great knowledge of Freudian psychoanalysis ...'

The electricity went off in between, and returned a little while later. The flow of talk was interrupted. *Mash's* face flushed a little. 'The situation here is very bad now. No idea at all when the electricity may come and go. We've mosquito-proofed the house, so they don't bother us, thank goodness! I stepped out just once, and there it was, buzzing right into the ear. I swatted it off—a mosquito! I caught it in a transparent bottle, drove to the Mayor's house, and strode into his office. I told him, "Here, I caught this from within city-limits, take a look!" The Mayor got the gooseflesh. "Sorry, *mashe*"—he said. He was so apologetic. I warned him. "I am not a citizen of this country. But I can file a case against you and your institution." I left only after stating that clearly.'

The phone rang then. He picked it up and started speaking straight—'Mr Vijayan, what are you all up to these days? This was a place once governed by leaders like E.M.S. Namboodiripad.'

I listened to him curiously. Then he put the phone down and turned to me. 'I gave him a piece of my mind. That was the CPM State Secretary, Pinarayi Vijayan ... he stayed with me the last time he came to the US. A nice person, though sort of rough on the outside—but that's because he's sincere. The chap is very fond of rice gruel and roasted pappadam for supper.' He chuckled. He was particular that his body should not know it even when he was laughing hard.

'There's no one from here who hasn't visited us at home in the US. Comrade Baby, oh, what a gem of a person!

Music, culture, literature ... there isn't a topic he's not familiar with! Another visitor was one Mr Ismail, from the CPI ... oh, he resembles the late Malayalam cine actor K.P.A.C. Sunny! You'd think he's crude, and a villain of sorts. But such a nice person he is actually! He's very fond of anchovies. I got a friend from Texas to introduce us, and he flew in. When he got to know that we had spent money flying him in, he was rather cross. He likes the simple life ... Oh, he's in the tradition of leaders like M.N. Govindan Nair ... Ah, to get back to the Madras Presidency College ... at that time, a relative of the low-caste Ezhava reformer and campaigner Dr Palpu, was a teacher there, a Mr Narayanan. So brilliant—when he came into class, it was like the sun had risen ... so handsome! There were not many people that fair among the Ezhavas those days. One day, something interesting happened ...'

Geevarughese *mash* paused to pour himself some more wine. Sipping it twice, he returned to the story energetically. 'Can never forget Narayanan, see, you can't even imagine ... he was in charge of the book club those days ... You should've seen him read books. One day I saw him reading Marx's *Das Kapital*—there was also a Mr Peethambara Kurup, who used to be a neighbour of our Marxist intellectual K. Damodaran. Nice guy! Clean-shaven, hair combed backwards, so dashing! They were reading it together and something happened ... a big thing. See I haven't forgotten anything! It was a Tuesday evening. I really blamed them for it—really harshly. But it wasn't on purpose. When they were turning the seventy-ninth page together, the page got torn, top to bottom. I lost control, I shouted. Of course, I had the good health to shout in those days, you know! I told them in no uncertain terms: "Do not repeat this EVER". They were both rattled.' Lost in memories, he closed his eyes and chuckled endlessly—taking care that his body did not shake even a bit. In the intervals that the laughter provided, he refilled the empty wineglass.

'You know, I am eighty-four now. Yet it feels like all this happened just yesterday ... what all political and cultural movements ... I had a subordinate who was active first in Subhash Chandra Bose's Forward Bloc and later in the undivided Communist Party—Mr Kurien. He was already an activist while in college. He'd lost two of his front teeth, having taken a kick in the face from the police. We were together in the hostel. He would bring banned journals and so on ... those days, the police smelt such stuff out. We used to discuss the internal complexities of the communist ideology. Kurien often forgot where he was. That's how it happened ... I'll never forget that day. He was crazy about boiled eggs, and in those days there weren't very many local shops selling them. See, one day he went down and bought ten eggs, and while he was crossing the road, he noticed a truck hurtling towards him ... some truck full of heavy sacks of onions or something ... and it was speeding. He jumped back and got off the road, and waited till it had passed. But what happened was something else, entirely ...' Geevarughese *mash* downed three or four more cheekfuls of wine and wiped his lips.

'That was Kurien, after all. A very absent-minded person! V.K. Krishna Menon was speaking at the Town Hall that day. It was overflowing with people, not an inch of space was free inside. I was there, and I saw the sight while I was returning. Kurien, whose attention was diverted by the enormous pile of onion sacks loaded on the truck, dropped four of the eggs, and they were shattered on the road. I was really shocked! I scolded him a lot—such absent-mindedness, really!

'Oh, the days of the Liberation Struggle! Weren't things really on a boil then! Who all were in the first Communist ministry? Lions, roaring lions, all of them! But the Congress activists managed to do a trick! I was in the hostel then. Used to walk to college. Then and now, I take a walk two times a day. Sleep, food, reading—all of these are well-planned, then and now alike! I have a monthly check-up done, without fail. Last time, my eldest son who's in California called Dr Vimal and set up the appointment. Haven't you heard of him— he's Nalapatt Narayana Menon's grandchild—by marriage I think. Very nice person. He was saying —if this is how it's going to be, you'll ace a hundred and fifty years! I laughed a lot—what a humorous chap! The only other person I have met who can crack a real joke like that is Mr Nayanar, the CPM leader. He stayed with us when he came to the US. He's quite stubborn about his daily dose of fenugreek seeds. And of course, crazy about the movies! But Krishna Pillai, a very serious communist. How luminous his eyes used to be! Poor soul, he left us early. And the other person to remember is Varghese, the naxalite martyr. If only he had been a little more disciplined in the communist party, he would have been chief minister now. I feel so sorry when I think. What did he get from becoming a naxalite insurgent?

He would have been an asset to the state, so sincere he was. A gem of a person.'

Letting out a long sigh, he got up and went to the loo. The maid laid out lunch on the table. He was barely back at the table after washing his hands, when the phone rang. He started in Malayalam, then moved to English. There were chuckles in the middle and gestures of surprise too. Then he replaced the receiver and turned to me. 'That was Antony, a very nice person. Very senior Congressman and Defence Minister, A.K. Antony. I had told him, let's not pick the Defence Ministry—but what was the use of telling him? But then you can't blame him either. It was the party's decision, what could he do? He never misses lunch at our house when in the States. Very easy person. Likes his rice gruel! Do we have many youngsters these days who are as simple?

'Ah! Just remembered—this was when the Punnapra-Vayalar armed revolt was in full swing. Oh, leaders like Comrade T.V. Thomas! Everyone had gone underground. I must have been barely twenty then. Hot-blooded! The newspaper arrived only very occasionally. The party's journal and notices reached you only after they passed through several hands, and so would be rather soiled! Though they would print only some hundred or two hundred copies in the stone-letter type, it would be passed between some two thousand people at least. I was reading this stuff and was intoxicated with the revolution. Immediate revolution— that was my position. I maintained a correspondence with a Mr Raghavan, who was a close relative of the legendary communist comrade R. Sugatan. He too was underground for some time. But then, the poor chap was beaten up so badly by the police that he fell ill with tuberculosis and died. We used to write to each other very frequently. Mainly about the party policy documents, our visions about the future, and so on ... One day I came to a decision. I felt that there was no point in hanging on to ordinary life anymore. I didn't turn around to look again, just went off to Alappuzha. The boat was to leave early the next morning. I touched Appan's feet—he was fast asleep—and took off. Who knew if I would ever return? I went straight to meet Raghavan. Had a hard time finding him. Was very risky—remember, the police were snooping all around. They could leap at you from anywhere ... I can never forget it. By noon, I found him. He was hiding in a harijan's hovel. We had lunch there. Excellent gruel and dry-roasted pappadam, and fried dried fish on the side. Oh, in my whole life I haven't had a tastier dried fish. After lunch, I set out for home and reached before evening, so I didn't have to face Appan's questioning. But I felt so guilty; I couldn't look at his face for a whole week. Ah, that reminds me of ...'

The phone rang then. Starting in Malayalam, then moving on to English, Geevarughese *mash* was dealing with some bigwig. He put the phone down and said, 'That's our Oommen. Our Oommen Chandy, the Congress leader. He called to share a funny thing he thought up now. Chandy was in Trivandrum and had stopped his car to get cloth for some new shirts. Yes, true, it is time he got some new shirts ready and waiting! Apparently high-quality *khaddar* has become so expensive now that he'll probably have to sell his family property! He couldn't stop laughing thinking of that!'

Geevarughese *mash* too could not stop laughing. When he was telling me the real reason for it, I got up.

'Okay, then, *mashe*, it's time now. I will come tomorrow ...'

He didn't like it, but let me leave. Before I left, he went inside and brought me a paper envelope. I knew. There were six thousand-rupee notes in it. This was my salary day. He had never failed in paying on the dot.

My family matters now proceed quite smoothly. But my wife says that nowadays, I am strangely forgetful. One night, she was really worried seeing me get up in my sleep and rummage in the waste-bin, looking for something. When she switched the light on, I apparently stared at her vacantly.

'What are you groping for?' She was on the verge of tears when she asked.

I allegedly responded with a question to her: 'Where is Geevarughese *mash* hiding? Have you seen?'

She hugged me tight and wept for a long time. The poor girl—how many years do you think it's been since she passed her MA in History? She's not been able to even register for her PhD. I thought of her plight and it made me weep for some time. But that also made me remember something else.

One day, I want to ask Geevarughese *mash*: Where are you present in Kerala's history? That extraordinary distance you were able to keep, even as you were almost omnipresent in it—how come we do not have a name for that fine art? In these new times—which are exactly of the new sort, without being really that new—can I take you as my guru?

THE LUNATIC

Mathabhranthan, they say in Malayalam. *Matham* = Religion.
Bhranthan = Madman.

But anyone would agree, lunatics have no religion. Disputes about time and country make no sense to them, either. The lunatic newly arrived in town had no religion, and no name, either. A small crowd, however, gathered around him and it tore off his dirty clothes, cut his beard and whiskers, pushed him under a public tap, and forced him to take a bath. They made him wear the nearly-new clothes of a young man who had died an untimely death. The crowd was not just of humanists; they were also respectable folk. So, it may be because of that, that they put him on a long-distance. Maybe the bus driver and conductor found him sleeping in sheer exhaustion in the last bus at the bus stand and had a long quarrel with him, and finally threw him out. Whatever may have been the case, he was behaving in a very familiar way in the town which was entirely unfamiliar to him.

Lunacy is a form of superstition. There is a happy ignorance in it which believes that it knows everything. The lunatic, irrespective of how much time may have passed, keeps adding his personal rooms and dining rooms and thinking alcoves to the broken architecture of his delusion.

The space-time of his reality hovered over actual reality and made everything lighter. Actually he could fit into his pocket a house, a whole building complex, why, even a large city! But hunger is different. It sinks its teeth into even lunacy. So the lunatic transported his spirit into a dog's sense of smell and wandered greedily through different parts of the town.

The search for food brought him to the front of a multi-storey building complex, recently inaugurated by a Central government minister and his cronies, in which many ultra-modern amenities, including wi-fi, were installed. The people there caught their prey directly through the satellite, but there was also a waste-bin in the front, which looked like a mistake. We have not yet become modern enough to tamper with the waste-bin, how fortunate! The senior telecom officer, Sarangapaani, had dropped into it the lunch his wife had specially packed for him in a banana-leaf. His stomach ache proved to be a blessing for the lunatic.

Overcome with joy, he retreated with the packet into a small bylane and wolfed the food down, sitting near a public tap. Why, he even let out a few burps, like a sane person.

The next benefactor was Sureshkumar K.K., an LD clerk who had been recently transferred to the Civil Station. He was already an expert in signing the afternoon register and disappearing from sight. He was hurrying towards a movie theatre showing a hot porno film and lighting a cigarette on the way. He was in such a rush that he didn't notice he had dropped an unlit cigarette from his case. Our lunatic was in luck. He picked up that expensive cigarette, got a light from P.M. Balakrishnan (receiver in the chitty-company in town), leaned on a half-wall painted with jewellery-shop ads, and began to smoke. As he was relaxing this way, suddenly, there was a huge explosion that made even the lunatic start violently. Suddenly hundreds of police vans, ambulances, fire engines and OB vans of TV channels began to dash hither and thither, silencing the steady chatter of the city. As people stood stunned, not comprehending, warning-announcements addressing civilians began to be heard.

'For the special attention of citizens:

Forming crowds or groups or raising slogans and organising public meetings in the city are hereby prohibited now through CRPC Section 144. Do not touch suitcases, boxes, radios, TVs, computers, mobile phones, etc., which seem to have no owners; please inform the police control room if you happen to see any such ownerless object. Please also inform the police control if you chance upon suspicious-looking behaviour or individuals. This is an announcement by the police ... For the special attention of citizens, forming crowds or groups or raising slogans ...'

The news that very destructive bomb blasts had occurred in many parts of the city spread everywhere in no time. People began to panic and run.

The lunatic smiled mildly, taking in the last puff from the cigarette. He whispered as though to himself—is there anything crazier than this?

DIG of Police K.M. Kuruvila, Jayaraj from the Special Branch, N.S. Swamy from the Special Investigative Team, the Crime Branch SP Nizamuddin, City Commissoner Jagjit, Vijayan from the Anti-Terrorist Wing, Home Special Secretary Vinulal, and the Head of the Department of Forensics, Dr Mathew Ulakathil—a special high-level meeting of these important people was on. The officer from the SIT, N.S. Swamy, was especially uneasy in the room filled with a mysterious scent. He was receiving calls from the Home Ministry in Delhi every five minutes: report within twenty-four hours.

Who was behind such an organised series of bomb blasts? Who was their final target? Information about the nature of the blasts, the earlier case histories of such blasts, and so on, was ready in minutes. The discussion which had begun at seven in the morning was still on at two in the afternoon and had really reached nowhere. Just when they had decided to continue after lunch and risen, the City Commissioner received an emergency message—from a thorough inch-to-inch search of the affected areas. A clue from the CCTV cameras installed in the front of the new building complex. A panning shot just four seconds long.

One of the fourteen blasts in the city had happened there. The forensic experts had identified the waste-bin as the place where the bomb had been hidden. What's the bearded man doing? Dropping the bomb there, or taking it? The scene was replayed several times ... it was still unclear. N.S. Swamy of the SIT exclaimed—'This's him, the Lashkar man! Play it again in slow motion. Is he planting something there or taking it?' After many replays, they were struck by two things: first, a packet in his hand, and second, he turned briefly in the act, casting a furtive glance at the crowd there.

'He's taking a packet, sir,' said Vijayan of the ATW, only to be silenced by a sharp look from N.S. Swamy—Don't fall for vague circumstantial evidence. Body language!

DIG Kuruvila supported Swamy from the other side of the table: 'Yes, why should someone either dropping or taking a packet be so wary and keep turning his face and moving his eyeball suspiciously close to the edge of his eye? Show the scene again.'

The bearded fellow froze in the close-up. Jayaraj, of the Intelligence Wing, reminded: 'Sir, look at the time-code? The blasts occurred exactly at 1:50 p.m. The perpetrator places the packet—the explosive—at exactly 1:17 p.m. He can reach a safe place in thirty-three minutes for sure. Makes sense. The only piece that doesn't fit is the LD clerk from the Civil Station who got killed, Sureshkumar K.K. They say he wasn't in office that afternoon; they also say he may have slipped out to watch a movie.'

'Show the close-up of the bearded chap again. When he turns, that is,' Swamy asked.

'Look at his features—rather Kashmiri, right? And of course, the beard.'

'Can't rule it out. He should be arrested as soon as possible.'

The message reached the city and its outskirts lightning-fast.

In four hours, Crime Branch SP Nizamuddin received a message: 'We have got him, sir. But we committed a blunder ...'

'What blunder?'

'The TV channels have got wind of it somehow. It's all over breaking news, and it's like a crazy crowd down here with the OB vans and everything.'

Nizamuddin was livid. Enough spies inside the department! Idiots! Now what all dishes are they going to cook up from this item?

Before the conference ended, DIG Kuruvila announced: 'He's the main link in this case. He should be questioned in extreme seclusion.'

Everything was set up in minutes. The interrogation team had six members: City Commissioner Jagjith, N.S. Swamy, Vijayan of the ATW, Vinulal, Dr Ulakathil from Forensics, and a new guest—the criminal psychologist Dr Koshy. Leaving clear instructions that the suspect should not be subjected to physical torture, DIG Kuruvila set off for other important official meetings.

The bearded chap was ushered into a room set up like a coffee-shop in a five-star hotel. Those in the room stood up involuntarily when he stepped in. Only the City Commissioner was in uniform. Seeing him, the lunatic gave an overstated salute, brimming with crazy enthusiasm and curiosity. Because he couldn't forget that this was a high-value suspect, the officer couldn't stop himself from acknowledging the salute.

N.S. Swamy greeted him warmly: 'Please come in.'

Surveying the suspect from top to toe for a moment and offering a gentle, almost coy, smile, he pointed to a very nice chair, gesturing to him to sit down.

Once he managed to sit, the lunatic's blooming mind awaited a shy bride-to-be bringing them tea and snacks on a tray. He was now seeing his bride formally.

'You didn't tell us your name,' Vijayan of ATW asked.

'Sorry about that—my name is Kilji, Allaudin Kilji.'

'That must be your nom de guerre?'

'Yes.'

'Where are you based in Kerala?'

The suspect asked them back: 'Where's the tea?'

Commissioner Jagjith asked for tea over the intercom.

'What do you want to eat?'

'Some rice?'

The criminal psychologist, Dr Koshy threw a glance at Swamy: This man is more dangerous than we thought. His general manner is of one who's confident that no one can make him talk.

'Kilji, where in Kerala are you based?'

'Have been outside Kerala for the most part.'

'Kashmir?'

'Yes, mostly there. Also learned how to play the game there.'

'Training too?'

'Yes!'

A tough nut! Dr Koshy marked that in his mind. An impregnable mind. Only third-degree might yield results. The cool, easy stare in his eyes is the scary borderland.

In the middle, Swamy got up impatiently: 'Look Kilji, we haven't taken an easy breath since last noon. Haven't slept a wink. It'll be better for us all if you tell us everything straight up. No need for introduction or adjectives.'

The first question: 'Are there any more explosives planted that are yet to explode? If so, where? The explosive, RDX, that is.'

Kilji now imagined himself to be in a movie. He is an underworld don. The camera is rolling—'Mr Inspector, don't ask me such silly questions like I were a kid. For underworld dons like me, this is just a trifle, a mere trifle!' He topped it with a huge guffaw.

N.S. Swamy lost control: 'Shut up!'

Silence in the room.

Kilji stopped guffawing and said: 'If you don't need this guffaw, let's do another take ... where's the touch up?'

'*Eda*, you are making fun of us! You know this department has many other means to make you tell the truth!'

'Come on. Mr Kilji, where else have you and your gang planted explosives? We nee' that info before we finth owt 'oo you are.' Jagjith's Malayalam was still unbelievably distorted.

'We know you are just a pawn in your gang's hands. Tell us, where else are the explosives?'

Kilji said: 'I'm hungry. Where's the tea? I will have the *porotta* and meat curry and then tell you.'

Vinulal glanced at the Commissioner and made to pick up the intercom. Then Swamy's mobile phone rang. The call was from the SIT office. The officer sounded like he was at his wits' end: 'Sir, the press, the channels ... sick of them! What am I to tell them, sir?'

'The pests! No comments, say that.'

'That won't do, sir. The assistant secretary from the Home ... right to info ...'

'Just tell them we are now looking for the main offender. By no means should his picture fall into the hands of the press.'

'Kilji, how many mobile phones do you have?'

'Where's the *porotta* and meat curry? I am famished!'

Criminal psychologist Dr Koshy looked at N.S. Swamy again. When they gave themselves a break in the interrogation and came out of the room, he told Swamy: 'This man is more virulent than we thought. Better get special permission from Kuruvila and try third-degree.'

N.S. Swamy was by now in some confusion: 'There's some abnormality somewhere, don't you think?'

That was a blow to Dr Koshy's ego. But he hid the annoyance and smiled: 'Sir, I think you haven't paid attention to my letterhead. My doctorate is from an American university ... in psychology. This man is feigning madness.'

American university, psychology—these two references shook Swamy awake. He quickly agreed with Dr Koshy now: 'I thought so too.'

After almost a day-long session of interrogation and third-degree treatment, Kilji revealed the truths one by one: the intense training he'd received from Pakistani terrorists; participation in the Bombay blasts; the futile attempt on the life of the Home Minister in Bangalore; the attack on the Parliament House. He also said that he was only feigning lunacy. And that there were stacks of heavy explosives waiting to be ignited in many parts of the city. The only thing he was unable to reveal was their exact location. At the end of very intense torture, he collapsed, murmuring 'RDX, RDX'.

In the early phase of torture, he had hit back, that's true. That was him trying to save his mentally unstable older sister from a gang that was beating her up in the street. He would wake hearing the *subahi* call from the nearby mosque. He'd studied in school and got her treatment from the income he made delivering newspapers. Once in a while, he would come to town to watch a movie. That was his only source of entertainment. Once, very unexpectedly, he happened to see a movie shoot. A sense of wonder from it had enveloped him for many days afterwards.

How carefully had he handled his sister's condition! But she still managed to evade him and get out of the house. She was fifty-five, but still those evil men had raped her. Slowly, he began to feel that what she said about things was true. His disquiet began to surface even in quarrels over unpaid newspaper bills. Very slowly, space and time tumbled upside down and began to toe his line. A house could be small enough to fit into his pocket. Perhaps a building complex too. Even a mighty city!

The fights over newspaper-bill arrears ended up with him getting seriously injured. He then attacked four hefty men from behind, but the police arrived. They flung a chair at the chest of the man who had no one to speak for him ... and now, here they were, beating him to a pulp.

He lay face down on the bare and wet floor.

Kilji. That name, now severed from Allaudin, was leaked along with his pencil-sketch to the newspapers. The TV channels hounded Kilji every second like stallions of war brushing their hooves impatiently.

Who is Kilji? The press wrote up his biography and drew up his astronomical chart. He became a hunted animal. Our feet comfortably up on the teapoy, while snacking on peanuts, we watched on TV—the Kashmiri terrorist. The reporter assumed the astrologer's role.

'Kilji allegedly arrived in town through the Beppur Port. He's six-and-a-half feet tall,' wrote one newspaper. 'Actually a dwarf,' claimed another.

The reporters secretly clawed at the policemen for news. Seeing the lead story in a prominent newspaper, the DIG called Swamy: 'What's this?'

'What, sir?'

'Of course, you have been allergic to the written word since long. Apparently, Kilji is a false name. He is not Muslim.'

The channels snatched that bit. Sparks flew in the panel discussions. The court took cognisance. Kilji would undergo a physical examination.

The investigative team asked for a week's time. His arms were bound to the sides and the parted legs too, so that any movement on the chair was simply impossible. The *ossan*, the barber who had been jobless for a long time, rubbed his rusted knife four or five times on the callus on his palm, before ripping the skin off the penis on that naked body with his left hand. The knife then closed its eyes in pain and kissed the skin.

Kilji cried out in bottomless agony: '*Amme, Pengale* ... Mother, Sister ... help!'

THE FLAMING PILLOW

Once there was a man who went mad. That was me.

I was sitting on the terrifying land's end of memories, lost in thought. It was then that Madness came to me, on magical feet, as a formless form, an essence-less essence. It asked me: 'Do you want to see the sky?'

I said: 'Silence! My mind now rests on the terrifying land's end of memories.'

It flitted around me on wing-less wings. In the valley, the shepherds and their flocks passed by.

I said to no one in particular: 'Last night, I had a dream. Two old goats, with their eyes gouged out, looked straight at me.'

Madness asked: 'Shall we go on a trip?'

I said: 'I want liberation.'

Madness said: 'I am both liberation and salvation. I sink in the blue lake and resurrect as the red mountain. I will make you as free as God. There, darkness will turn into a tree of light. You will be solid and liquid at once. The cry that no one hears will emerge from the left side of your throat as a lock, a curl of song. There is no Time there, no memory either. No solid and liquid. Yet it will all be present. Come.'

I felt a very close kinship with Madness. But I could not help saying, 'Can't you see? I am in chains. Four or five blackened fetters, wild and pathetic, bind me to the rocks.'

Madness then turned into the dying day. Dusk came up and stood behind me. Shorn of bodily organs, I was now just a mind. Madness said to me: 'You cannot escape me. All evenings are the primal form of Madness.'

The human souls that passed through the valleys became mere lanterns. Helpless, I wept. I tried to pull over myself the earth's coverlets. The topsoil crumbled scornfully. Madness put its hand on my shoulder. It made me sip the goblet of weariness.

When I woke up, it was day. Madness had left. I saw the walls and the iron bars crowd on the earth like a jungle. They had sprouted in the pitch-dark of the night. The earth's iron railings pressed deep down into the nether world. How was I to face this?

Then, he came: 'Do not fear. I am with you.'

I tried my best but could not suppress the words: 'You are a pitiless usurer. A soul who revels in the pain of others. You will give light and in return, take away my eyes. You will give sound but demand my ears.'

Madness paid no attention to my words. It said: 'Today is a lovely day. Take some sun. Let your muscles cramped by the night's chill relax a bit. Let us go for a walk.'

I said: 'I am not coming. You are a contagious ailment. You are the pox with iron nails in its throat, extending an eager embrace. Go away. Let me lie in the blue lake for a while. Let my soul find comfort in the earth's warm springs.'

Madness left me of its own accord, turning into air quickly.

I was liberated. I spoke intelligently with other human beings. I could move fast now. But now, I am tiring very easily, too soon. The human beings on this earth appear to me an unfathomable sea of greed. Their talk and their moves are nothing but the lashing waves in that sea.

I walked away. Within my loneliness, my peace was like a self-igniting pillow. Madness arrived and doused the flames. I told it: 'I do not understand the logic of this earth. I have had enough of trying to compromise with and be amicable towards it, trying to swallow, stifle and suppress my own self.'

Madness replied: 'I am inviting you to the other world for a brief while.'

Biting down my pain, I asked: 'Friend, I am asking you, is there Reason on the other side? Not the Reason that celebrates aggression. I think Reason's logic has swelled into a huge mob, which is now attacking me.'

'No,' it said. 'In the world we are going to go to, there is no Reason, no logic. But no unreason or illogic either. There you can tear your body apart and entrust it to an iron-carriage dashing towards it furiously. You can pass into painless liberation. There, the cruelties of love do not exist. Nor does the wildness of desire. No dishes there that endlessly stoke hunger. Now, tell me, where will you stand?'

It continued: 'Between life and death. There are people there who, stripped of organs, wander wretchedly, and wail and weep. I am at times the flower-soft shower of compassion, and at other times, the cruel downpour of venomous snakes. I break the ocean to make snake-clouds, and the clouds, to make showers of venomous hatchlings.'

'Where do you come from?' I asked.

Madness laughed. 'You are still in the world of Reason. Come, shake Time off your feet; strip off the self-consciousness from your body!'

I asked it again: 'Is your world at peace?'

It replied: 'I am the devil who waits on the path to God. Often when people burdened with hardships and dilemmas and wounded by Reason pass this way, I creep up behind them just for fun and slash their throats. Then I rush back at the same pace and heal the cut instantly. I take the terribly shaken person out of Time, make them feel that they are asleep, and then let them wake up ... I can go anywhere in this world. Except into sleep, long or short.'

Once someone went mad. That was me. I did not see Madness fully and properly. Even the questions it asked sounded like answers.

Putting out a lantern, that had been obtained after a lot of effort, with a single puff, it asked me: 'What do you seek?'

I said: 'I seek God who stays hidden.'

Suddenly it raised its hands magically, and, lighting the lantern in a way that it flamed like a torch, asked: 'What about now? Who do you seek?'

I said again: 'The God who stays hidden.'

Madness kicked the lantern out of the way. Its eyes were not aflame with anger. It walked away in a measured rhythm. It then grew enormously into the sky ahead. After a moment's mysterious smile, Madness tore apart the sky before it. Then, in a voice slightly tinged with frustration, it said: 'All right. You may go. There is no meaning in caring for you. God awaits you.'

WINTER

Whenever I see whole pieces of ginger that aren't crushed to be blended into the meat curry, and the misty mornings of the month of December, I remember Asainarkka. Asainarkka, who was sane for nine months and insane for three.

Our village, with paddy fields stretching endlessly like the sea. Have you seen the December mist cloaking endless expanses of paddy land? The dawn before the sun rises. There is a certain light that is born upon the earth just before dawn. It is very faint. Like the dim shine you'd get if you oiled the blackness of the dark. Come into our fields in that dimness, and you can see dead people standing in a crowd. That's what our grandparents have told us. Who among them would you like to see? Fix your mind solely on that person, and your eyes on the mountain of mist congealed in the fields. It's possible that they may even wave at you desolately.

I am now coming to Asainarkka.

Our village was rudely awakened by a red-dirt road that strode through the very heart of the paddy land and split it. Not sure when that happened. It wasn't anything beyond the exciting prospect of a road in summer, and in the rains, just a disgusting mushy ugly path. In time, it became a part of the fields in our eyes.

Asainarkka was the first person to wake up in the village each morning. Only if you get up at Asainarkka's hour and start walking can you catch the train from town—there was even such a saying in our parts. Every day, he would walk clutching the staff of early dawn. There was a rhythm to the sound of his staff hitting the smooth stones on either side of the red-dirt path (what all meanings did it bear!).

Asainarkka's whitish, rheumy eyes and silence-covered ears would be alert. His nostrils would be flared. Is there a light somewhere? The murmur of a crowd? What was that smell, like frankincense? No, that was just a feeling. The rhythm of Asainarkka's staff. Searching, again and again. Alertness. He's groping, searching, for death. Death. It intoxicated him. If it flashed even a tiny bit somewhere, Asainarkka would exult within. He searched for it all the time. Its scent. Its touch. Its endless rest. Its intoxication. Diving and swimming in it, breaking free from worldly concerns. We would be in our huts, tumbling in the madness of slumber. And then, the sound of a staff going tap, tap, tap. It would stamp on the head of the slumbering consciousness itself. For sure it was not a sound that bore the meaning of death alone. We would start at the sound and grope our own bodies, many times. First, one's own body. Then that of relatives and friends. Everyone would seek the other. You'd have asked—are you awake? Or you'd have felt like asking.

But no one hated him.

In our village, there is the practice of offering a feast of ghee-rice and meat curry on the fortieth day after a death in the house. It is called the fortieth-day feast. On that day, the friends and relatives of the deceased gather and pray for the departed. A small pandal is erected in front of the house. Plastic tables and chairs are arranged beneath it. We eat the dead person's ghee-rice and meat curry on them. Asainarkka never missed a single such feast. No one had to invite him; he would be there. First, his shadow on one side of the pandal. Then his rather long head, raised high. The intense sparkle in his whitish eyes. The rough patches of greying beard on his face. He would look as though he'd just gone to yet another fortieth-day feast. Hundreds and hundreds of them, really. Still, his hunger stayed unquenched.

My Muthaappa had passed away; it was I who served the rice at his fortieth-day feast. Asainarkka was wolfing it down at a steady pace. The shape of his little finger caught my eye. It looked like a piece of ginger, with a sixth finger growing out of it. While the five fingers scooped up the rice, the sixth alone stayed apart!

Everyone in the pandal would fall silent when he entered. Was it respect or suppressed hatred or bulging helplessness? It was hard to tell.

Everything would change when the mist arrived. Asainarkka would go mad then. Many would feel relieved at that; others would sense a loss.

He would set out in the middle of the night on which the season of the mists began. As though on a journey no one could stop him from making, he would pull out a coat and a cap from his box that reeked of age, wear them, and step out. He would abandon his staff. His gait was generally erect, but now it would become more so. The boundless earth of the midnight mist, unreachable from the ditches in the field. He would stand in the middle of it, clap, and call: 'Come, come, come.'

That would bring, no one knows where from, innumerable puppies who would surround him. He would take out pieces of leather from his bundle and make a collar for each one. He would then build a fire in the middle of the field. The puppies would cuddle close to him, warming themselves by the fire, like grandchildren.

He'd sing for them—'Come, come, come.'

In between, he would get up, turn round and round, and clap, calling them.

Hearing this from our huts, we would tell each other: 'Asainarkka's lost his marbles again.' Rarely, someone would say: 'It's winter.'

During winter, he would wander all over the village with the puppies in tow. He would sleep anywhere. Sometimes on someone's verandah; sometimes in a firewood shed. His presence would catch someone going out to pee at night totally unawares and they would scream in fright.

During the time of madness, he paid no attention at all to human beings. His attention would not only be focussed on the puppies, but he would also show love for the crows and the calves. He would chop up food for them. The crows would happily peck at it. The puppies would tumble in and out of his coat playfully. Some mischievous crows would perch on his shoulders and drop pieces of appams into his pocket, like loving gifts.

How did he collect all this food? No one knew. Pulling out a packet from his bundle, sitting down on the path by the fields, he'd call out to them—'Come, come, come ...'

He used to be in the army during the time of the British. There, one winter, he went mad. One wintry midnight, he got out of the camp and walked away. He had taken a horse with him. How far they must have walked!

One night, we heard: 'Come, come, come ...' The news spread in the village like sunlight: 'Asainarkka is back. There's a horse with him!'

'Ah, the white man! Will he spare anyone?'

The days passed. The horse grew emaciated. It did not get enough to eat. It had no place to live. But it stuck by Asainarkka. He spoke to it in some strange language. Massaged it with oil; washed it in the canal. He fed it horse-gram.

One day, quite unexpectedly, the soldiers came. When they came to know that Asainarkka was mad, they spared him. They tried to take the horse away, but it would not go. In the end, they had to take Asainarkka too to make it go with them.

Many winters passed. Asainarkka went mad and became sane in turn. We would know of winter's end by the tap-tap-tap of his staff falling on the stones by the red-dirt road. He would give up the puppies totally when he became sane (by then they would have grown mostly). The crows wouldn't come close to Grandpa Asainar then.

Hearing the tapping sound early in the morning, we'd tell each other—ah, his madness is gone. Others would say—the winter has passed.

In the mornings after the winter was over, householders looking out of their homes would be surprised to see Asainarkka at their doorsteps. A lanky man who stood erect.

The whitish eyes and the jagged voice. 'Where is my ghee-rice?' he would ask.

That's when the householders would remember the head of the house, the lady of the house, the infant, son, daughter—any family member who had passed away during the winter.

He would not budge an inch without getting his share of ghee-rice and meat curry. He'd lay his claim on the fleshly rice of death as a right. Who could challenge it? It was unchallengeable, this right, like death itself.

Sometimes, in very rare moments, he would turn into a loving grandfather. When I was very young, in one of those moments, I had asked him: 'Asainar Uppappa, how do you get so many puppy dogs in the winter?'

'They come out of the mist, chekka.'

'How do you get their food?'

'Chekka, the mist gives that too.'

What more to ask, really?

'All right, where do you get the horse-gram for the horse?'

'Your father's father's father's father gives it to me, my son. He was a horse-gram trader.'

'You mean, from more than a hundred years back?'

'Yes. I met him in the mist. He asked if you were well.'

Sometimes he would pass on news from the dead he met in the mist. Sometimes, he would not answer a single question. He would simply glare or pretend not to hear.

I managed to corner him once at a lighter moment. He was by himself, absorbed in thought.

'Asainar Uppappa, how did my grandfather die?'

My grandfather died when my father was just a year and a half old, of dysentery. There were suspicions raised about his death. He was known to be a large-hearted man. The first child born among a group of settlers who had moved into an island called Pambiruthi. The family was very wealthy. He was the only heir. Their lands rolled far beyond where the eye could reach ... He was to manage it all. But my Uppappa did not care for any of it. He was perpetually on a bamboo tree-house, making up songs all the time, like a new challenger in a make-up-a-song contest. That life passed away in a hurry, swimming lustily on the music of a made-up song. He never ate or drank on time, never saw his wife. He became the master of the *kettuppattu*, making up songs and stringing them. Daring the rival masters, his youth danced in the strength of poetry.

> *Valiant youth, flying on the wings of music*
> *Don't you want to reach the Mashra?*
> *Don't you want to make a retinue*
> *To go wed Moon biwi's girl? ...*

The sharp arrow would seek the rival master's weakest spots. He could not but lose. Sitting in his tree-house, Uppappa would make them shit in their pants as they ran in shame. The local grandees brought many famous song-stringers from many lands, rewarding them with gold, to challenge his poetic powers. All of them lost and ran away in shame. The talented can summon money. But money can't summon talent.

'How did he die, right? All right, I'll ask when I see him.'

I forgot to remind him. He too didn't tell me.

Many years went by.

In the rat race to survive, I left the land of the rolling paddy fields and lived alone. The season of mists came into my memory in rare moments. Also, Madman Asainarkka.

When did I see him last?

At Kunhahmed's Uppa's fortieth-day feast.

I was seeing him after many years. He was eating the *neichoru* with the same zest. The server's hand ached from serving him pieces of meat again and again. He didn't refuse. Like the unending hunger of death, he kept devouring the food. People kept giving him chisel-sharp looks as he ate. Asainarkka picked up the piece of coconut-frond stick and cleaned his teeth. I looked just one time into his eyes. *Chekka*, don't you want to know how your Uppappa died, they seemed to be asking.

Why do you need to know? I asked myself.

For revenge? To get even? To break a leg? Why?

From where was I to find the grit to answer these questions?

Many times, when I came back home, early in winter mornings, I would see him and the puppies in the field warming themselves at the fire. And later, the tap-tap-tap of the staff hitting the stones and making small talk. Many holiday seasons passed after this. On one such day, I heard that Asainarkka had died. The night before. I searched my memory. Yes, the night before, too, I had heard the staff's tapping rhythm. Quite possible, we may hear it again.

What else but a coincidence! I was present at his fortieth-day feast. I was bound to. The pandal was up.

Friends and relatives were moving about briskly, serving the rice and meat curry. No one was eating their food with relish. They were turning around constantly to look—hasn't he come to partake in the fortieth-day feast? This is not wintertime, he may come. He may ask for his share of rice and meat. In these parts, we expect him whenever we open our front-doors.

A huge man. Head held high. Whitish, sharp eyes. Thick greying clumps of beard on a dark-skinned face. The winter, too, will come.

ISA

The police jeep zoomed up the road till the junction that turned towards the Manapparamb village and braked suddenly. Two passers-by with freakish hairdos stared, startled, when Sub-Inspector Phalgunan leaned out of the jeep and gestured to them. 'Where is the house of Keelath Tarvi Hasan, the freedom fighter?'

The freaker-style youngsters looked puzzled. Yes, they remembered 'freedom struggle' from the PSC exam coaching. But knew nothing more.

Sameer, the constable who was sitting in the back of the jeep, leaned forward and said, '*Saar*, I know the way. We have to go straight ahead. Turn left at the second turn in the road. There's a tall tree there. A dirt road runs behind it.'

The driver changed gears, relieved.

Sub-Inspector Phalgunan threw Sameer a look. He then asked, '*Edo*, does it say anywhere in your religion that the dead may come back?'

Sameer answered modestly, 'No, *saar*, there's no such belief. After the burial, a few large stones may be placed on the *kabar*. Then a prayer is said. Sometimes a few twigs of henna are planted at the head and watered.'

Phalgunan seemed lost in thought for some seconds, and then said, 'Hmm. Anyway, this thing's become a huge nuisance.'

'*Saar*,' Sameer agreed.

'He disappears right before your eyes. That family is absolutely on edge. The son-in-law of this allegedly-deceased Isa, he is very close to the MLA! He insists that this Isa is lurking somewhere around the house.'

When the jeep turned left at the second turning, dusk had slowly begun to fall. Kasim stood at the gate of the house, waiting with a large torch in hand. He had several busy shops in town to run; today he had left them early to be here.

The high-pitched cry of a fox could be heard from the patch of wilderness behind the house. The jeep went past the gate and reached the part of the large yard laid with interlocked tiles. Kasim, who had been hurrying behind the jeep, came up with a respectful smile and spoke with the SI: 'The MLA called just now!' It was clear from his expression that SI Phalgunan did not like this. But he quickly got down from the jeep and took a good look at the premises which the wilderness seemed to be taking over.

Kasim said, 'Ammosan, my father-in-law, was spotted first near my mother-in-law's room. He was calling out, "Amina, I'm not dead, please open the door, once. I am hungry, thirsty, I want to see our children", he was weeping and wailing non-stop.'

'Ammayi—that means your wife's Umma. That is, the wife of your allegedly-deceased Ammosan, right?'

'Yes, *saar*.'

'Maybe she imagined it? She's after all a widow who loved her husband deeply back then. Not surprising at all.'

'That's what we too thought, *saar*. But I saw him too. He peeps from the jungle behind this house. His face looks as though he were crying. I get scared and throw large stones at him. Then he disappears into the wild.'

Phalgunan *saar* thought for a short while. He looked again and again at the dense verdure behind the house.

'It's confirmed that he died in Dubai, isn't it?'

'Yes, *saar*. Covid wreaked havoc in the Dubai Naif and other parts. So many Malayalis died. You must have read in the papers, *saar*.'

By then the tea and snacks had appeared in the drawing room. The policemen sat behind Phalgunan, somewhat subdued, and helped themselves to these awkwardly.

'What work was he doing in Dubai?' SI Phalgunan took a bite of the banana fritter and asked Kasim.

'Odd jobs. He did odd jobs there to support this family. Tell you the truth, this family is really the fruit of his self-sacrifice. There he didn't even have a proper room—and that is why he caught the Covid virus. He'd come once in two years; only then would he get a new shirt for himself! It was only then that he got a decent shave! More than forty years without his family! It was an awful life there, *saar*. Then he turned sixty and did not renew his visa, and was about to return for good. That's when Covid struck hard. The truth is that I feel terrible, having to do this. It is totally wrong to do this. His life was the very picture of sacrifice. He married an orphan without a paisa for dowry. His father was a freedom fighter, born in a prominent family—he left home for the freedom struggle at the age of eighteen. The British confiscated his house and properties. He believed firmly that all of it would be returned to him after Independence. But no! He was in and out of courts till the end of his life. Some crooked official had written a note claiming he was a citizen of Pakistan! Apparently, a technical error! He collapsed in the court and died. Isa was his only son; he fed the family washing dishes in a teashop. And he was not a clever chap, either.'

'*Ayyo*, so why are you stoning someone who worked so hard for his family? Why are you chasing him away?' Phalgunan looked unsettled.

'*Saar*, how to let someone who's dead into the house?'

'Is the record of death correct?'

SI Phalgunan fiddled with a heavy electric torch, scanned the house and the premises carefully with a long look, and asked again, as if preparing for something big.

'Are the papers reporting the death in order?'

Kasim quickly stepped back into a room and came out with a neatly arranged bundle of papers.

'Yes, *saar*. Was buried somewhere in Dubai. No details about the site of the grave are available—but it was somewhere in the desert. His younger daughter's husband was a witness.'

Phalgunan signalled to his men to search the premises. Then handing the bundle of papers back to Kasim, he said, 'Yes, they seem correct. Attested by the Embassy.' He fixed a look on Kasim's face, still flabbergasted, and asked, 'Maybe it is a madman who resembles him?'

'No, *saar*, it is our Ammosan, Isa, for sure. He wept aloud when I aimed a stone at him.'

'What?'

'That he had indeed died but wanted to live more. "I have never yet lived," he said. "This is my land." When I heard that, the rock I was about to hurl actually quivered.'

'And then?'

'I asked, "Your wife who saw you risen from the dead was terrified and has now taken ill—is feverish. Your children and grandchildren shrink in fear. Can't you go away, live somewhere else?" "This is my land, where else am I to live," he kept whispering for many minutes.

'I said, "However, those with you here are the living. Remember that. Why can't the dead stay with the dead? If you ruin our peace, I'll have to stone you! Please don't make us do this evil deed." And saying that, shaken by a wave of emotion, I began to hurl stones at him. One of them hit his forehead, just above one eye, and wounded him. He began to bleed and held his face in unbearable pain ... not sure if it was a cry or a grunt, but he disappeared into the wild again.'

Phalgunan could not help plunging deep into thought. Then he said, 'Let me tell you straight up, Kasim. This is more of a human issue than a legal one. The living grabbed everything they could and have now abandoned him at the border of death, right?'

After a long sigh of guilt and helplessness, Kasim replied, 'The MLA said that there is no legal issue here. The law is only for the living and their dependents. *Saar*, the law books say nothing of the dead. They should be buried. They are not citizens, they have no passport, no Aadhaar card, no voting rights. They have nothing, *saar*. That's what the High Court lawyer also told us. At the least, the dead should be under the ground. The MLA agrees too. What is the point of destroying the peace of the living this way?'

'MLA' being a dirty word that was an occasional nuisance in the limits of his power, Phalgunan suppressed a yawn with the back of his hand.

The policemen were now back from the search.

'He isn't anywhere there,' Phalgunan told Sameer. 'Didn't we see a firewood shed behind the house? Search carefully around there. Let the rest of the group search around for a second time.'

Suddenly, the growl of an animal enveloped the murkiness there. It had by then submerged the whole house like the inscrutable enigma of life after death. In the sky, a strange deep blue and an even more mysterious red smouldered. The beam of the torch moved frantically through the yard, twisting and turning, searching, for a long time. No one found Isa. The birds which were until then chirping and cooing, singly and together, fell silent, as though by a common decision. When that round of torch-light search was over, Phalgunan walked carefully towards the decrepit firewood shed on the western edge of the yard which was surrounded by uncannily wild thickets.

Opening the termite-eaten door that had no bolt, Constable Sameer entered the shed. He was confident because he held a torch that let out a powerful beam of light. He checked all the corners, and then focussed the beam on the firewood stacked there. The stack was nearly ten feet tall. He climbed up to take a look, helped by a colleague.

Between the dilapidated roof and the stack of firewood, there was hardly any space for a man to sit. But he thought it wise to check there. However, another truth is that a scent that seemed to be mediating between life and death had actually urged him to look there. His guess wasn't wrong; in the sharply falling beam of torchlight, he looked up, stunned—Isa! A strange animal-like wretchedness mirrored in his eyeballs. The eyeballs gleamed with the desire to live, with the expectation of life. Isa had been sleeping there. His dirty clothes were even more dirty. The sunken cheeks, the protruding cheek bones, were like a desolate desert filled with thorn-bushes.

The silent exchanges of eternal time passed between them in the snap of a finger. Did Sameer spend more time than necessary there? Did he look too keenly? Suspecting something, Phalgunan called from below, 'Is he up there?'

Sameer had no doubts whatsoever.

'No, *saar*, no one here.'

Phalgunan said to Kasim, 'He must have run away seeing the police. Won't come again, probably.'

Saar, are the dead still afraid of the police? Kasim wanted to ask him.

Phalgunan sent the beam of his torch around again and said, 'What sort of a wilderness is this, Kasim? Have you made a vow or what, to let the jungle take over this compound?'

Kasim then told him that private thing: '*Saar*, the truth is that it has been cleared often. But whenever that's done, that very night, it will rain here. The very next day, it would all have grown right back.'

'Very strange things, indeed,' replied Phalgunan, after a few moments of thought, to no one in particular.

'And we did try to sell this house and move elsewhere, but even that isn't working ...' Kasim paused abruptly, and sounding absolutely helpless and tormented by a moral dilemma, he blurted out: '*Saar*, is it possible to file a case against a dead man?'

Not knowing what to say to that, Phalgunan did not respond for many minutes. After some thought, he replied, 'Come to the station and file a complaint anyway. You must let us know if there are any developments.'

Sitting in the vehicle preparing to leave, he seemed immersed in thinking how to comfort Kasim. Then he said, 'Let me see if there is some rule that will let us send out a search warrant for a dead person.'

*

When all the world had gone to sleep, when the pouring and unbroken showers wiped away even the dark violet signs of dawn with a relentless black hum, Sameer appeared once again at the shed. The raindrops got past his raincoat even, and fell on his chest. He had felt that the night that was passing belonged to a solitary soul. He had turned and tossed, unable to sleep, and then arrived at a decision.

Sameer stood below the stacked firewood and called out softly: 'Isaakkaa, come down.'

Woken abruptly from his stupor, Isa stared, startled.

'I won't harm you. Please come down here.'

From the firewood on which the tree-scent of the sawmill and the wetness of the mud lingered—firewood which carried within it the prickliness of death—Isa climbed down, by himself. He took every step warily, looking at Sameer with suspicion.

'Please believe me. I promise, I do. You won't be harmed.'

The water for the tea boiled on the stove at that unearthly hour in which all consciousness seemed to be numb and slumberous. Sameer mixed tea and sugar expertly and brought it to Isa, who still seemed scared.

Isa said, 'I don't want the tea. Can you please reduce the speed of the fan? I'm cold.'

Sameer switched off the fan and asked, 'Shall I give you some clothes to change into?'

'No.'

'These white clothes are so dirty! How did you manage to climb up and lie down on that pile of wood, Isaakka?'

Isa laughed without laughing. The rust of memories blended in that laugh.

'We were fourteen people in a single room in the Gulf. Each got two hundred dirhams. The rent went up again. I climbed up to the third row of the stacked beds, for many years, to sleep. In the beginning, we had floor-level iron beds. Then those disappeared. That side-street in Naif in Dubai became a city for poor people like me so quickly! It was a market, filled with the sounds of street-sellers bargaining. As the city grew, the biggest concern was living space. The space for us to sleep shrank each day. But when we thought of the hardships back home, we just forgot the shrinking of our space.'

Sameer listened. Isa continued to talk. 'If you woke up at night thirsty or wanting to pee, you just had to hold it in till morning. You had to be careful not to hit your hand against the ceiling fan! In the beginning, it was very irritating to see the fan there. Then, gradually, its hum began to speak to me. In a voice that swung and shook, the fan told me stories from back home. That the girl I had loved had eloped with a southerner who went there for some work. That my wife was sullen because I was late in sending letters. The renovation of the house started yesterday. Everyone says your older daughter looks just like you. Hey, the well-digger Govindettan came yesterday and decided on which spot to dig the well; will need to dig at least twenty rings down to find water. Our daughter Pu won the first prize in the singing contest in her school. Her teacher Krishnan came home to tell us that she must attend singing classes; I have never seen a girl sing so well in my whole life, he said. Usman Haji from the mosque committee came over to object—singing is *haraam* and Krishnan teacher is a *kafir*. Uppa, this is Pu … we don't need the harmonium that you planned to buy for me.

'A room with twelve cots; one took turns to shit, bathe, everything. There was a queue even to cry. In the Gulf rooms, they give you a heavy, soft blanket. When I covered myself with it, I would imagine my dead mother hugging me. When you heard the water from the bathroom tap fall without a break into the bucket, you could guess—someone was weeping in there.

'This land was made possible by those tears, hidden by the sound of the water gushing out of the tap. Marrying off sisters, building houses, digging wells, replacing the leaking wooden roofs with concrete ones, sending children to

English-medium schools, giving birth in private hospitals, wearing decent clothes, moving around in decent vehicles, giving rise to colourful marketplaces, hearing the air conditioner's hum. Even the Gods got decent homes and robes because of us, including the ear-splitting music played there every evening. When we sought to get everything that we viewed and desired from afar for our families, their brimming happiness was our greatest asset. This urge to make our families happy—it drew us on an on, like an intoxication! Yes, a never-ending illusion. We never lived—we just kept amassing everything, everything. Someday, we would come back here and live ... *Saar*, does my death in the middle of this disqualify me?'

Though a strong man, Sameer could not hide his sighs. 'Kasim threw stones and hurt you a lot, didn't he?' It was Sameer's need—he needed to cut across time with that single question.

Isa said, 'The dead man's wounds are shared by all those who joined in killing him.'

'Did you really die, Isaakkaa?'

Isa laughed. 'You are seeing me. What do you think? Didn't your Uppa also die like this in Saudi Arabia one day?'

The memory of his father made Sameer's mind broil, and he forgot Isa. When he woke up from it, Isa had left. The rest of the questions he had for him felt so childish now.

When the police jeep reached the house, the news spread like wildfire. That turned out to be a bigger nuisance for the family than the dead man himself. At his wits' end now, Kasim went to meet the MLA.

Thinking for a while, the MLA, a man who liked to plan his moves, said. 'There's a brothel in my constituency. Let us send our fellows there and tell them to claim that they spotted a ghost there. Everyone will rush over to that side. That's how our news industry works, right? We should bury news with other news.'

Rolling over that last bit of the sentence in his mind, he laughed, enjoying his own words. 'At least for some time, the price of land in those parts will fall. I'll then buy some land there in your name. Two birds with a single bullet!'

Kasim smiled.

Outside, a companion crow balanced itself on the back of a grazing cow.

'We have much to learn even from these living creatures, Kasim.'

Anyway, that trick worked. The attention of the locals and the news industry shifted to ten kilometres away. People began to forget the ghost-infested house of Keelath Tarvi Hasan.

But Isa still hung back, showing himself now and then in the thickets that the rain periodically summoned back to life. He tried to enter the house many times, but failed. Kasim and Chempakam and the kids even wounded him seriously, thrusting through the window a sharp bamboo pole. Fear and loud cries haunted the place, offering no respite.

'My daughter, Chempakam, please open the door! I will be caught outside in the rain. Please, I just need a mat. And just that green-bordered blanket that I brought from Dubai when I came the last time. I am dying here of the cold.'

The truth was that the daughter who lay face down sobbing on the cot, loved him a great deal. Every time her Uppa returned from the Gulf, once in two years, the spring-time cuckoos would gather on her fields of joy. There was no road back then. Seeing Uppa come up the mud-ridge on the field, carrying his big suitcase on his shoulder, was the ultimate joy, distilled from life's very essence, dripping with honey. Before he reached, the wonderful fragrance from inside his suitcase would reach her. When the suitcase was opened, Sainaba—whom her father lovingly called Chempakam—would turn away shyly.

He had got just two days of leave when she was given in marriage to Kasim. When he was leaving the next day, Uppa wept like he was going to pieces.

'Chempakam, my daughter ...' his voice had broken.

He clasped his younger daughter, Pu, close. Pu—he called her that. It meant 'flower'.

She was really small then. 'Uppa, don't go,' she had sobbed. And he had wailed, calling out her name. That cry, as painful as though the flesh had been torn off the bone, now swept back there like wind from the desert and waited at the edge of the soul's fields.

> *Oh wind of Miraj's nights,*
> *Oh wind that cools the desert,*
> *That enters the heart,*
> *Quivers in the sea.*
> *Oh wind that dips in coolness ...*

The *mappila* song from a cassette Uppa had brought back then broke out in her memory, weeping. Chempakam banged her head as she wailed in agony. Her husband tried to comfort her: 'What's the use? However dear they may be, how do we let the dead live in the house?'

She stammered through her tears: 'Can't we give him that dark room near the shed? He'll stay there. I'll take care of my Uppa!'

'Don't be crazy! What are we going to tell the police when they come seeking him? His name isn't on the ration card. He has no Aadhaar card. No passport either. The police will get him ...'

Isa stretched his arms through the window and begged, 'Give me some water from our well, my daughter. Uppa is thirsty. My dear, *mole*, Chempakame ...'

Chempakam held close his arms through the window-bars and fainted. In the examination room, the doctor told Kasim, 'Kasim, you are not an ignorant man. This is psychological war. The mind of the dead one is not what you think. If you let the dead into the house, all of you will die—the patient and the baby.'

Turning towards Chempakam who lay drained, the doctor said, 'What's in the past is in the past. Love is not the bag of dirty laundry three times your weight that you must necessarily lug around.'

When she wailed aloud again, the doctor pointed towards the baby sleeping beside her. 'Who do you want, your dead Uppa, or this child who is just beginning to live? You have to decide.'

She whispered amidst the sobs: 'My child.'

'Good. It is possible that the police will arrest and deport Isa. The dead are gone. Try to live pretending that you haven't seen anything. The world is the garden of those who agree. If not, even the soil under your feet will slip away.'

At the end of the phone conversation, from many thousands of miles away, Pu told her sister, 'I won't come now, *ithaa*. I can't see Uppa dead.' Then she cut the call.

When the faithful had salaam-ed each other and parted after the *Asr namaz*, Karim stood diffidently beside the *khatib* of the mosque, Kunhalikkutty Ustad.

'Who? What is it?'

'The family of Keelath Tarvi Hasan.'

'Who?' He did not comprehend.

'The freedom fighter, Tarvi Hasan.'

'Fighter? What's that?'

Kasim tried to invoke the name of the famous freedom fighter Ali Musliyar of Malappuram.

'Ali Musliyar? He's still the *khatib* at Chembathotti in Talipparamba? All right, whatever. Tell me, why have you come?'

'My father-in-law was in the Gulf, some forty years. He died of the pandemic there. Was buried there too.'

'Oh, that is that Isa's house! Have heard of it. He's dead but not gone, eh?'

Kasim suddenly felt very emotional. 'No, he hasn't. Is there any way ...?'

Kunhalikkutty Ustad did not hesitate to think even a moment. 'It'll cost you some money. You'll have to get the senior ustad from Ramapuram. It's the Shaitan who's come to your house. Not Isa or Yesu Christu.'

After the nightly prayer and dinner, Kunhalikkutty Ustad went to bed in the room on the side of the mosque. He, however, jolted awake at midnight, dreaming that someone was shaking hard the iron bolt of the door of the mosque.

Not able to discern time and space, the ustad was stupefied for a moment. Then he switched on the light and decided to take a look, just to allay his fear. He opened the door. Someone was there.

'Who?'

The man did not wait for permission; he came in. 'It's me, Isa,' he said. 'The son of Keelath Tarvi Hasan. I worked for forty whole years in the scorching desert and got seared inside and out. I died there.'

The ustad paled; he did not know what to do.

'I am no Shaitan or Iblis, just raw human being. Please don't side with them in evicting me from my land! Who are you with in decisive moments like this one?'

Kunhalikkutty Ustad could not hold back his anger. 'I am with God, of course! A dead one like you is Iblis, what else? Get out of the mosque, you devil!' He was snared by fear now, and trembling, he began to chant prayers in a mumble.

Isa said, 'This mosque, this sacred house of God, was built with my money too! With many dirhams made by deferring my own desires. What will you get from throwing me out of this land upon which I perform the *sujud*, my prayer? Job security? Honours?'

The man was now quaking with fear.

'Don't shiver. I'll chant you a prayer. I was ill with the pandemic, and they put me in a half-finished building. In the middle of the desert. There were, however, people there who were still compassionate. Ordinary people, plain folk. They helped me. And then, there was just the hiss of the desert wind! I will teach you the prayer that I hissed into my chest in the middle of the fever and chill— *Subahnallahi alhamdulillaahi vala ilaaha illallaahu allahu akbar vala haula vala khutva illaa billaahil aliyyil aleem.* Rabb is compassion alone in life and death, and after death. *Ar Rahmaanurrahim*!'

'I won't go there, will that do?' The *khatib* nearly peed as he uttered these words.

The next morning, after the *subahi* prayer, Kunhalikkutty Ustad picked up his bundle and hurried back in fear to his native village of Krishnapuram. He did not even notice the drizzle. He kept chanting, '*Subahnallahi alhamdulillaahi vala ilaaha illallaahu* ...' The fringes of his faith were crumbling as he nervously turned around, looking for the Shaitan and angel.

The new police superintendent was an old pal of the MLA's. The MLA was generous when he was in a crisis. So he was one of the first people the police superintendent phoned after taking over office. Two kindred souls in the worldly universe.

'Tell me, what is the issue? What should I do?'

Pointing to Kasim who was sitting by himself in the backseat, the MLA introduced him: 'This is Kasim. Has been with me for many years. He manages many of my businesses, in truth. But recently, he's been rather off. Can't blame him, I'd have been too, if I were him.'

Kasim sobbed within.

'What happened?' the SP asked.

'Domestic problems.'

'Oh!'

'Kasim's father-in-law was in the Gulf for some forty years. Died of Covid there last month. They buried him there too. Now he is back.'

'Didn't get you.'

'The dead man has come back.'

The SP laughed. 'Will anyone in their sound mind do that?'

'It's serious, *saar.*'

'Okay, okay.' The SP became serious once more. 'It's a case of impersonation, isn't it?'

'No. The death has been confirmed. By one of his sons-in-law who's in the Gulf. He is a witness to the burial!'

'So not impersonation. It would have been easy if it were just that! What if there's been a mistake in the name or some detail on that end?'

'No.'

Kasim had by then brought him all the papers.

Examining them carefully, the SP said, 'The papers are *pucca.*'

'What if this son-in-law has been up to some hanky-panky?'

'We checked. And besides, the greater burden from Isa's arrival would be on the family here. They aren't capable of any such operation. Just harmless folk!'

Kasim began to butt in with his troubles.

The SP leaned back in his chair, let out a sigh, and said as though to himself, 'Completely illogical! The cleared thickets sprouting back in a single night's rain? What's this? A Hollywood horror movie? Wounds from stoning healing in a day? A whole police station has been after him, but no use!' He turned to Kasim: 'Say, Isa hasn't picked up any magic, has he?'

Kasim had been hanging back, wanting to say something more.

The MLA signed to him to speak. Encouraged thus, he spoke: '*Saar*, these days my father-in-law isn't alone.'

'Then?'

'Familiar-seeming faces ... But I can't remember, exactly. People whom we have seen in the school history books ...'

The SP said, 'Strange indeed! Maybe it's a mass illusion. Like they make the Taj Mahal disappear ...'

'But if it is real, then how do we deal with it?' The MLA wanted to know.

The SP thought for a while, swinging his legs back and forth. Then he said, 'A case must be filed.'

'On what grounds?' The MLA stirred in his chair.

The SP smiled. 'Do the police have a problem there? To cook up something? If it is real then Isa must be caught. The Special Force must surround the wild area behind the house.'

'Such a big operation will need ...'

'Yes, reasons will have to be given. And strong ones. We have to plan well. It must be connected to national security. That's the only way to do it. And in a way that's correct too. He is not alive, officially, and so not any more a citizen of this country. Has no recorded citizenship, either. So he has absolutely no rights whatsoever. He has to leave this country at once. We'll pass an order demanding his papers. He can't produce them. That means we have the authority to hand out any punishment—including expulsion. Under the new circumstances, the courts will support us. How are the dead to possess documents! This is an illegal entry!'

He played with the paperweight on the table and added, 'Do you know what the biggest crime in this world is?' Pausing for a few moments, he answered his own question: 'Illegal migration!'

The MLA gaped at him.

Then, putting the paperweight in its place and rotating it, he said, 'You have no papers, so you have migrated here—says the government. If the individual has no proof to the contrary, he will have to leave. For somewhere else. If possible, for the netherworld.'

The MLA was now diffident, left without words. 'The elections are due. This should not affect me in any way,' he cautioned.

And thus, all the scriptwriters and directors in the news industry woke up. The sketch, the route map, the spying, the channel discussions. 'Who is actually the person reported dead in this News Hour? Will the dead come back, or reincarnate? Will science win, and humanity be defeated?'

In the end, the paramilitary forces surrounded the wild thickets. 'Isa, show yourself, come out now,' the policeman announced many times through his hand-held microphone, aiming it at the layers of darkness in there. The birds that had been chirping away till then suddenly looked down from the boughs of the trees and fell silent.

When there was no sign of movement, the announcement began to grow harsh and hostile: 'Isa, show yourself, come out—you are staying there at your own peril. If you do not come out, we will have to arrest your wife and children.'

At that, a sorrowful sigh emerged from the jungle. Slowly, Isa's face became discernible from amidst the intense green of the leaves. 'This is my land. I cannot leave it even if I die.'

'There's a government order. We know that you aren't alone in this drama. If you don't surrender, we will have to shoot. You will die.'

'Will the dead be killed again? If so, do kill all those who are with me, *saar*!'

Suddenly, all the trees and shrubs in that jungle stood up straight. They grew limbs. The birds rose up from them, screeching in protest. They became one, and it was impossible to tell apart people from the wild and the birds. In a second, the jungle grew enormously. People of many castes, faiths, colours, languages, clans, rationalists, people from many lands, poets, the bards of love ... The jungle just grew and grew behind them. A mighty ocean of the wild!

In the middle of this, some fool hollered: 'Fire!'